MISTER
ROBERTS

ALEXEI SAYLE
MISTER ROBERTS

SCEPTRE

First published in Great Britain in 2008 by Sceptre
An imprint of Hodder & Stoughton
An Hachette UK company

2

A CIP catalogue record for this title is
available from the British Library

ISBN 978 0 340 96156 8

Typeset in Sabon MT by Palimpsest Book Production Limited,
Grangemouth, Stirlingshire
Printed and bound by Clays Ltd, St Ives plc

Hodder & Stoughton policy is to use papers that are natural, renewable
and recyclable products and made from wood grown in sustainable forests.
The logging and manufacturing processes are expected to conform to the
environmental regulations of the country of origin.

Hodder & Stoughton Ltd
338 Euston Road
London NW1 3BH

www.hodder.co.uk

For Linda

Contents

Next Summer in London

The summer air was thick and viscous, like the poisonous water drawn from polluted Chinese rivers that was used to fill up the souvenir snowdomes of London laid out with the rest of the tat on the shelves of the tourist shops. Laurence strode purposefully through the West End, though by now he knew he was far too late for the meeting. He admonished himself over what a stupid waste of time it was to fly all the way from Spain, spend an uncomfortable night on his cousin's fold-out bed, get a train in from Brockley that was so small and cramped it seemed like a half-sized model of itself, and then not to get to Soho House at the appointed time.

Laurence told himself he was being melodramatic

saying that snubbing the producers of a TV series, who'd been considering him as their costume designer meant the end of his career. After all, it wasn't absolutely certain that he would never, ever, work again. On the other hand, even in the television business where people could, in this play-it-safe century, still be pretty wayward, turning up for the interview was generally considered a basic requirement for getting a job. And everybody said you didn't upset the people connected to the particular, diminutive star who was attached to this project. Short, light-entertainment stars were inclined towards being highly vindictive: everybody in the industry was aware of the story of the young runner who'd spilt a tiny amount of soup on Charlie Drake – a strange comedian who'd been big in the sixties – and was more or less blacklisted. The runner had ended up taking a job as a traffic warden, though subsequently he was able to ticket Charlie's Rolls-Royce up to five times a week.

Laurence was in two minds over the prospect of not working: up until a few months ago, he would have considered it a catastrophe. Back then, his sense of himself had been completely tied up with career success, but each day he felt his former ambition recede like the ache of a healing wound. In some ways he missed his old unhappy self, as if for many years he had lived next door to a football stadium that had recently moved, and now he was nostalgic for the noise and mess and the men peeing in his front garden.

He was more certain that he never wanted to return to London. It had been over four years since Laurence's last visit and during that time surveillance cameras and chain coffee shops seemed to have grown and expanded like bathroom mould. From where he stood now at a road junction completely blocked by one of the incredibly long buses that had appeared since his previous trip (he wondered whether you didn't just get on one and then walk to your destination so seldom did they seem to move) he could see two branches of Subway, two Pret a Mangers, three Starbucks and twenty-one video cameras on fat black poles. Laurence couldn't shake the idea that travelling through modern London was rather like being trapped in one of those cartoons they showed on the TV when he was a kid where, if a character was running, the background would go round and round on a loop behind them, the same few objects flashing past time after time. Laurence had always resisted the temptation to moan about the state of the UK in the way so many expat Brits did. He'd always had the vague feeling that to disrespect your own country was to disrespect yourself in some fashion but he had to admit that London seemed like a sordid mess to him now.

All this wasn't why he hadn't gone to the meeting. Laurence knew for certain that the reason he hadn't shown up at Soho House was to do with what had occurred in his village in Spain over the Christmas holidays. Even though it was now early summer, since 'the Events' he'd had a great deal of trouble taking the idea of work seriously. Money might become a bit of a problem in the future but he liked the idea of being frugal. He thought he might get a plot from the town hall and grow his own vegetables.

There was only one high and difficult hurdle that had to be got over before his new thrifty life could truly begin. It had been at the back of his mind in Spain shouting to be heard but since he'd been in London it had grown like a government sub-committee. Laurence had this overwhelming urge to tell somebody, anybody, every detail of what had happened. If he lived in a normal place he would, perhaps, be able to discuss it with those who had been there, but in Spain there was something called *el pacto del olvido*, literally the 'pact of Forgetting'. It was an unspoken and collective decision taken after the death of Generalissimo Franco: the only way Spain could survive the end of fascism without succumbing to savage retribution, as had happened in so many other countries, was by a tacit, communal agreement never to talk about the awful incidents that had taken place. The foreign community in his

village over-enthusiastically adopted all things
Spanish, so they too had taken on their own *pacto
del olvido*, which over the years had come to en-
compass a lengthy list of things which they could
never discuss. The events Laurence had the irresistible
compulsion to talk about were currently at the top
of that list.

Laurence supposed this need to unburden himself
was connected with him being out of the valley for
the first time since it happened. After all, it was
something many travellers did. Liberated from home
and amongst strangers whom they had no chance of
seeing again, people were often overcome with an
irresistible desire to tell another person their darkest
secrets. Over the years Laurence had had men and
women in airport lounges, hotel bars and train
stations relate to him the most intimate and
disturbing confidences: how they were in love with
their sister, how they binged on jam, how they'd sold
nuclear material to Chechen separatists. Now he
wanted to do the same thing, but the problem was
he didn't have any idea who to talk to. Whoever he
confided in needed to accept certain far-fetched
things as being true. If he didn't choose carefully
there was the danger that some stranger might
pretend to accept the things as being true just to
humour him but really think he was deluded. That
wouldn't be nearly good enough. He was certain he'd

pick up if they were humouring him, and then he wouldn't get the sense of release he so desperately craved.

Right at the moment he was thinking all this, Laurence noticed the man standing in the middle of the pavement not twenty metres away: poised as if he'd been placed there by one of those interventionist deities people prayed to, an all-powerful life form who cared whether or not they passed their cookery exam. Laurence knew at once that here was somebody who he could easily tell his whole story to. This man would regard as true everything that the average stranger in the bus station waiting room would think were the ravings of a delusional psychotic.

With what he thought was a big friendly smile on his face Laurence approached the man. He was younger than he'd seemed from a distance, with black, unkempt, curly hair and skin that was a waxy white, even though he must spend a good part of the day outdoors. Up close his eyes were bloodshot and darted from side to side as if he'd once lived somewhere where there were a lot of wasps. His suit seemed too big for him and the wrinkled white shirt he wore was cinched in at the waist by a ratty leather belt.

At first the young man seemed a little surprised to encounter such eagerness, Laurence assumed that usually he had to do at least a little cajoling to reel a contact in. Never the less he seemed gratified by the interest and invited the older man to step inside a nearby building.

Despite its rather home-made-looking interior the place was dark and cool and fiercely air-conditioned and Laurence immediately felt the sweat evaporating from the small of his back. He thought that no matter how things went he could still be grateful to get in from the street. Soon they were sitting facing each other across a plain wooden table with a little clear plastic cup of chilled water beside each of them.

'So you say you have a story you wish to tell me?' the young man asked.

'Yes, indeed,' Laurence replied.

'Many have a story they need to get off their chests and I'm here to listen. Don't be afraid, there's nothing I haven't heard before.'

We'll see about that you pompous little prick, Laurence thought to himself, but said, 'It was like a miracle, seeing you there on the street.'

'A lot of people say that.'

'Hmmm. Perhaps not in the way you think but I've been longing to tell this story to somebody, anybody, for, well it seems like such a very long time. Even though it's only been a matter of months since it happened.'

'And what's been stopping you?'

'I had the idea that no ordinary person would believe it, but then like a vision I saw you just now and I thought, "Of course! He'll understand, he'll understand every bit of it. This is one of the few people in the world who will know that all of it is true.'"

'Of course,' said the young man, leaning forward and lacing his fingers together in a gesture of insincere solemnity. 'Please, do go on.'

Noche Buena

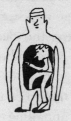

All the lights had gone out in the Valley. A terrible fierce wind had been blowing since the afternoon and as darkness fell, the power lines that brought electricity up from Granada to these Spanish mountain villages swung together touching. The resulting explosion sent clusters of sparks falling into the olive groves, producing a number of small fires and causing the fine new street lighting with built-in stereo speakers that the mayor had only just had installed on the road to the village to snap into darkness. From across the street, where he sat on a concrete bench inlaid with mosaic tiles, Stanley saw the lights go out in Bar Noche Azul and felt the sudden absence of its two TVs and one stereo as they yelped into silence.

The bench was uncomfortable to sit on being shaped like an angel lying on its side and weeping blue mosaic tears. It was a terrible pastiche of the work of the Catalan architect Antonio Gaudí. The mayor had had it built last year, to commemorate those who'd been murdered in the village and surrounding area during the civil war. Following the election of the socialist government after the Madrid bombings, the old pact of forgetting was beginning to break down. Slowly mass graves were starting to be uncovered and monuments, generally in appalling taste, had begun to appear up and down the valley.

Stanley supposed Simon wouldn't be coming now, seeing as he'd already been sitting on the uncomfortable bench for an hour and a half. Simon was, or had been, his best friend, an English boy in the same class of thirteen-year-olds at school. The plan had been that they were going to meet outside Bar Noche Azul, walk about for a bit, then go to Simon's house to play Halo on Simon's XBox 360. Stanley knew other kids at school who hung round in a big gang and had loads of what they regarded as close friends, but he'd never been like that. Certainly he had a few other mates but his inclination was always to have a special best friend whom he hung out with all the time. This was not the same special best friend, because there always seemed to come a point, like tonight, when the best friend badly let him down, then Stanley got really upset and they never spoke again.

He didn't know why Simon had abandoned him on the bench shaped like an angel on its side. Stanley remembered a time not that long ago when he had just done stuff without thinking about it, without reflection. Then, at some point over the last year or so, he had become aware that things happened for reasons. He thought of those reasons as shadowy indistinct shapes behind a gauze curtain, because although he knew now that reasons in a general sense were why things happened, he didn't know the specific reason why a particular thing happened. Why had Simon stood him up? Was it because Simon's dad talked in the third person all the time, said things like 'Daddy's been a bit of a nana, hasn't he, Simon?' Or was it because they'd just got a new washing machine or because their front door was blue? It could be any of these things as far as Stanley could tell.

He experienced a pang of loneliness that felt like he was on a long dark waterchute at a closed-up theme park; he wished with all his heart that he had a best friend right now to go down the long dark waterchute with him.

There was this new kid at school who really worried him. One day, six months ago he had turned up in class, his name was Runciman Carnforth. This boy, who was about the same size as Stanley but more muscled, with freckled pale skin and his hair in ginger dreadlocks, had lived with his parents as part of a religious cult that occupied a rambling farmhouse on the other side of the Granada-Motril motorway, in the foothills of the Alpujarras mountain range. Just as these rocky gorges and shaded valleys had once hidden the last Moors of Spain so they now housed all manner of lost tribes. Along the dry, stony river bed that ran down through the mountains there was a long sinuous bend where it looked as if all the old post office vans of Europe had come to die. In the backs of these ex-Bundespost Mercedes and Royal Mail Sherpas there lived teeming families of hippies, while below the village of Bubión there was a teepee village equipped with 8GB broadband access and outside of Trevélez there was a yoga centre made entirely out of car doors.

The Spanish were remarkably tolerant of these communities. They found their behaviour no more bizarre than that of the foreigners on the coast who drank themselves into a stupor then lay out in the sun until their skin turned to pork crackling. To them all foreigners were children and as such were not responsible for their actions. They kept an eye on them, just as they kept an eye on their own offspring – allowing them to put themselves at risk, balancing on a tower of chairs in a restaurant or running around traffic-packed squares and then swooping in at the last moment to bring them to safety almost ninety-five percent of the time.

Runciman's group had been one of those that had managed to avoid being noticed for a long time, so that when they'd finally been raided by a special anti-cult squad of the Guardia Civil, the damage they encountered – both physical and psychological – was severe. A lot of the women and their children had been rehoused in a block of municipal flats near the motorway, others had gone back to the UK and most of the male members of the cult were now in the state prison outside of Cadiz.

Though Runciman had gone around punching and kicking a lot of other kids he'd shown no sign that he'd even noticed Stanley existed. Still Stanley couldn't stop himself worrying that at some point Runciman would notice him and then the bullying would start just like you saw all the time on the TV. After all, he was the perfect target. You couldn't throw your weight around at school with the Spanish boys because of their big protective families and if Runciman picked on a really vulnerable British child nobody would respect him, but if he bullied Stanley, a boy who wasn't unpopular but wasn't that popular either, he'd solidify his status as boss of all the British kids in his year. Stanley wished sometimes he'd just get on with it so they could become bullier and bullyee.

Another confusing thing from the world of adults was that his mum was friendly with Runciman's mum. Stanley couldn't understand how she could be mates with a person who was parent to such a monster. But what really got Stanley down was the thought that he never swam across Runciman's consciousness. It made Stanley feel horribly small to know how little he mattered to the person who was ruining his life.

The microwave in Laurence's kitchen ground to a halt midway through spinning its radiation dance, right in the middle of heating up a Marks & Spencer's Cous Cous with Char-Roasted Vegetables. The ready meal was a Christmas present from his flight-attendant friend, Stuart, who was now asleep in the big bed. He'd brought it out from England, safe in the fridge of his Monarch Airlines flight from Luton to Malaga, which had landed that very Christmas Eve morning. This chilled package, gift-wrapped in soggy gold paper had been driven for two and a half hours on the back seat of a little red hire car up into the mountains. 'Happy Christmas, Laurence,' Stuart had said and kissed him, and Laurence had acted grateful, since it was what he'd asked for, but he thought to himself that really it was an empty pretence, this supposed longing for ready meals from the UK. It was the same nonsense as all of the British in the village saying the only thing they truly missed from home was a good curry when they didn't really, it was just something to say, something they had said for years. If they'd wanted to it was only an hour's drive to the city or the coast and then they could have as much curry as they wanted so why then did they never make the trip?

Of course, one reason they never took the journey was that nowadays most of the coast had the appearance of a new super-purgatory that was being built because the old one was nearly full. From Almeria to Malaga and beyond, a mighty highway under a permanent cloud of bitter smoke wove between gigantic concrete developments over which hovered towering cranes that dipped and grabbed like invaders from Mars in an Edwardian novel. From time to time the highway passed neurotically neat golf courses that sucked up all the water for hundreds of miles around, and near Marbella an Irish estate agent with the features of a baby-faced Ukrainian assassin had had giant billboards erected that stated, alongside an enormous picture of himself, 'You are now entering Mulverhill Country. Holiday developments in Spain, Dubai, Slovakia, Zimbabwe.'

Near Torreviejas there was a supermarket called 'Spainsbury's' that only sold products imported from Britain: shelf after shelf of Branston Pickle and boiled white bread and chipolatas made from mechanically recovered pigs' rectums. In Laurence's imagination it looked like an exhibit at the Imperial War Museum all about rationing during World War Two.

What truly kept him away from the coast, though, were the *plasticas*. Huge swathes of the hills inland from the sea were ruined by a continuous canopy of plastic. It covered so much territory that it could easily be seen from space, the roofs of fifty thousand closely packed plastic greenhouses. Just ten years ago this was largely uninhabited desert, rich in plant and animal life but arid. Now, under cover, tomatoes, lettuces, melons and peppers were grown all year round for the supermarkets of Europe. And they were expanding, moving rapidly north towards Laurence's village. You knew another one was going to be built when the diggers arrived to scar the hillside. They came pushing all in front of them, destroying mountainsides and blocking up dry riverbeds.

The plants in these humid hells would never touch soil – they were grown from bags, while chemical fertilisers were drip-fed to each plant from giant computer-controlled vats. If you went anywhere near them you'd notice a chemical tang in the air.

Laurence felt guilty about how much he hated this new Spain because as a Brit who had moved there, in a tiny way he sensed he was responsible for it.

He imagined sometimes that he had brought the contagion with him like a well-meaning missionary to the Americas whose blanket was heaving with smallpox. Whenever Laurence visited the hypermarket in Granada he saw a reminder of the damage the Spanish empire had done. In Carrefour, avoiding all the yelling, bright-red Brits falling over each other in the booze section, Laurence would find himself in the Productos Latinos Americanos aisle. In contrast to the clamour in the rest of the store a strange reverential silence always seemed to reign in this canyon of tins and jars, due to the little Inca-looking people who gathered there. Laurence guessed that they were Ecuadoreans, Bolivians and such. Workers from the *plasticas*, earning the lowest wages in Europe, who lived in camps of flimsy huts of cardboard and corrugated iron next to their workplaces and who had escaped to the city for a few days. The little Indians didn't ever buy anything, but he supposed fingering the packets of corn tortillas and jars of jalapeño peppers reminded them of home. Sometimes there seemed more to it though, their silent contemplation of boxes of enchiladas and tubes of chilli sauce appeared to have an almost religious quality to it, as if they were looking for something or somebody in the stacks who would lead them out of the land of their enslavement.

* * *

On that night, after the power cut off, Laurence slid open the heavy wooden door that led to the patio and went out into the shaking, windblown night to stare up at the suddenly revealed stars, stars which were normally hidden by the glare of the hundreds of powerful streetlights that the mayor was obsessed with installing. One of the things Laurence valued about his village was that there would never be any balsamic vinegar or lemongrass in the shop there. Twenty different kinds of ham certainly, but never anything that would not have been sold in the locale fifty years before. Unfortunately, this conservatism did not extend to modern technology. He remembered when he'd first come to the village nineteen years before. There'd been no street lighting and the stars in their billions had been on show every night; now the power cut had made them visible for the first time in ages. He stared hard at the blackness and the dusting of heavenly bodies and took the opportunity to try to feel insignificant. Laurence had heard people say that the sheer uncountable number of stars made you feel tiny and meaningless when confronted with the uncaring and infinite vastness of the universe. He figured that if he could only feel a little of that vastness then he might not mind so bloody much about the costume-designing job on the big new BBC-produced Henry James drama series being given to one of his younger rivals, he might not find Stuart quite so annoyingly dim and he might not feel that if he didn't do every sodding thing for the British community in the village then it simply wouldn't get done. Laurence tried hard to look into his soul to see if he could find some insignificance but there wasn't any there. Hey ho, he thought, trying to be relaxed about losing the TV job.

For a while, a year or two perhaps, work had been gradually tailing off; the gaps between projects getting longer and longer but this series going to somebody else meant he wouldn't have done anything for well over nine months.

It was what happened: he was getting old. Of course, in his time he'd pushed out an older generation of costume designers without a thought for how they felt and now the same thing was happening to him, all the thrusting young directors and producers who'd started out with Laurence were now organic sheep farmers, in long-term psychiatric care or were commissioning editors and channel controllers and so didn't make programmes anymore, indeed this last group were, in a way, more detached from TV than he was. If he still lived in the UK he might have been able to mix with the new batch of producers, go with them to rap concerts or skateboarding or whatever it was that they did for entertainment, but from high up in his valley it was impossible. Laurence thought to himself that in the new year he was going to have to return to the UK and make a really serious effort to get back in the game. If he just took a few meetings, chatted up a few old friends and looked up some of those godchildren he'd neglected then the quality of his work would shine through and get him the jobs he wanted.

Half a mile away a rocket rose in the night sky and exploded with a cascade of sparks, the muted boom reaching Laurence a few seconds later. He hardly noticed either. At any time of the day or night at more or less any time of the year there were explosions in the air above his valley. The locals would tell you that the firing of the rockets was connected with religious festivals or somebody's saint's day or the European Year of the Dyslexic but everybody knew in their heart that the impulse to fire them came from a deeper and older place. The hissing smoke trails, the bangs and the bright flashes of light were their way of frightening off devils. That in the dark, creeper-strung canyons and rock-strewn flatlands of the mountains there lurked beasts capable of unimaginable evil was accepted by all, and making a loud noise and a flash of light was considered the best way to keep them at a distance. Rockets were such a central part of life in the valley that most people kept a stock of them in their larder next to the dried spices, cured sausage and preserved peppers.

But then, as Laurence stared up into the black night sky, a more spectacular stellar display dragged him from his self-pitying reflections: one of the myriad of stars suddenly seemed to swell until it was as big as a tennis ball and brighter than one of the big 20k lights they used at Pinewood Studios. At first he assumed it was another projectile, but unlike a rocket it didn't die in a burst of sparkles. Instead the big burning ball hung seemingly only a few thousand metres above him, then abruptly lurched sideways across the sky. Rapidly diminishing in size the intense point of light finally disappeared behind one of the foothills of the Sierra Nevada.

A bright star shining over the village on Christmas Eve? Laurence thought to himself. My dear, how tacky is that? Then, with a sigh, he went back inside to Stuart.

Laurence was wrong. The bright shining light that had passed across the sky in front of him was not as he'd thought a shooting star – it was a burning spaceship. For several hours on that Christmas Eve, over on the dark side of the moon, an Imperial cruiser of the Galactic Empire had been battling with attack ships of the Universal Rebel Uprising. Time and again the tiny rebel fighters darted in, stinging the bulky lumbering battleship with their guns and missiles.

Most of the aliens on the big cruiser stuck to their task with brainless devotion but deep in the entrails of the ship one of the crew was feeling a great deal of fear. In appearance, like all his comrades, he was small and stocky, about a metre and a half tall, strong muscular arms and legs covered in greenish/grey scales with clawed hands and feet, his head longer than ours but with eyes, golden in colour, at the front – the mark of the predator. Inside, though, he was different from his fellows, he had a terror of death that had been bred out of most of his race. This alien's role on the ship was to monitor the condition of the defensive shields and to effect repairs on the shield generators as they sustained damage from enemy fire. With the knowledge his job afforded him he'd known for some time that the battlestar's defences could not take much more of the assault and once the shields went down the ship was finished.

He cursed the fact that through some accident of genetics or lack of conditioning he did not subscribe to the Imperial cult of cold rationality whereby an individual life was worth nothing and everything had to be sacrificed for the collective well-being of the Empire. He was convinced there was no eternal honour in dying for the common good as the Imperial political commissars endlessly stated, and he had devised a desperate plan not to.

A power surge from a missile strike caused an overload that exploded his bank of instruments, a flying shard of metal slashed him across his body, creating a gaping wound. Quickly, and without a backwards glance, he abandoned his post.

Clutching his side the alien began to shuffle into the fume-filled corridor, towards the outer hull of the ship some two kilometres away.

Over the following hour the deserter journeyed, with determination and stealth, the entire length of the crippled battlestar. He sped along moving walkways, he hissed from one end of antigravity chutes to the other, his molecules were disassembled then reconstituted as he teleported short distances and finally he ran down some stairs. At last he fetched up at a door in a distant corridor marked PLANETARY EXPLORATION SUITS. AUTHORISED ENTRY ONLY. After a quick, cautious look around, the alien slid inside.

The room he'd entered was bathed in a tranquil blue light and though it occasionally shook with the nearby impact of incoming missiles he found it strangely peaceful. As his eyesight adjusted to the gloom the alien saw far into the distance row upon row of bulky forms, each standing on its own plinth. These were the Planetary Exploration Suits. In essence, each outfit was a full-sized, fully powered replica of the inhabitants of various worlds that the Empire wished to explore without alerting the native population – a sort of cross between a gorilla suit, a deep-sea diver's outfit and a hollow cyborg. Through an access panel in the rear of each costume its operator could climb inside and once installed was able to activate it, to lift things and move about.

The alien deserter passed between the racks of lifeless forms, through their open access panels he occasionally caught a gleam of metal, a brief sight of glistening rods and highly polished swivel joints and a shadowy suggestion of inert dials and screens. The deserter knew he didn't have much time, the faraway screaming of the ship's engines told him the end couldn't be long in coming, but he also knew panic wouldn't help so he tried to remain calm. The alien was looking for one particular suit. As he searched he passed – amongst others – a large tentacled beast, a three-metre high tusked, bear-like animal, and an insectoid creature with enormous crab-like claws before he came to the entity he was looking for.

This Planetary Exploration Suit was the perfect replica of a member of the dominant species on the primitive planet above which the battle was now being fought. It stood in its storage tube immobile and lifeless – the figure of a big, muscular, earth man in his mid-forties. Its hair was deep black, brushed back from a high, intelligent forehead, its skin lightly tinged with olive. In the days to come, though everybody was able to agree that as a whole his features were broad and handsome, nobody was able to agree on greater detail, as if to each of them he presented a different face.

The man was dressed in a smart dark suit of a lightweight material, a white shirt and dark tie, such as might have been worn on earth by a man who frequented jazz clubs in Montmartre forty years ago – the time of the aliens' last visit to the earth.

The deserter pressed a button at the foot of the tube and with a hiss the glass cover rose into the roof. Looking round one last time he began to climb inside the humanoid. First he wriggled his legs into its legs then slipped his arms into its arms, squirmed his entire body inside the machine and finally fitted his head into a head-shaped space at the top of the man's chest. Once he was completely inside, the access panel closed with a snap and the interior of the machine burst into life. In front of his eyes a full-colour screen lit up, on which were displayed the exterior view, as seen through the camera eyes of the robot and grouped around the edges (like a head-up display in a fighter plane) various read-outs and images, such as external temperature, infra-red night vision, power reserves and so on.

Next, the alien began to experiment gingerly with movement. He tilted his head and the head of the robot moved, he moved his arms and the arms of the man moved too. Satisfied, the alien took a step forward and the man in the business suit strode clumsily off his podium and walked unsteadily out of the room.

In the time that the deserter had been in the Planetary Exploration Suit Room the condition of the ship had deteriorated rapidly and she was now in an extremely bad way. As the alien in the robot suit crept along the corridor the concussions grew worse, flames and gases spouted from ruptured pipes and exploding machinery, occasionally the big man would have to step delicately over the body of a crew member. Eventually the robot came to another door marked SHUTTLE CRAFT BAY, this one guarded by a single nervous trooper who didn't see the big humanoid leaping at him until the last moment by which time it was much too late to raise his weapon or cry out before his neck was broken by a single blow from the power-assisted arm of the robot. Without pausing, the alien opened the door to the shuttle bay, dragged the body of the guard inside and closed it behind him.

He was now inside a large hangar within which were several small space craft, stubby, inelegant little vessels used to ferry personnel between the battle cruiser and nearby planets. The man climbed into the cockpit of one of these craft and started it up.

Outside the Imperial cruiser the battle raged fiercer

than ever. The ship was taking hit after hit and while its laser cannon caught numerous attacking fighters, sending them spinning away in a thousand fragments they were instantly replaced by other incoming craft. In the midst of this fury the stolen shuttle came nosing out into the heat of battle from an exit hatch. It hung for a second on the skin of the mother ship, then with a burst of its jets, powered away from the fighting at top speed.

Soon the battle was left far behind, and in minutes the tiny ship reached the edge of the Earth's atmosphere, the alien relaxed a little and began to consider what he was going to do next. It dawned on him that he hadn't really thought through his escape plan that thoroughly. While he'd been obsessed with getting away from the doomed ship he hadn't considered how he was going to live on this foreign planet; from the reports he'd read on the ship's central computer he knew that the atmosphere was breathable and that with a few dietary supplements he could eat the food, but he wondered what he was going to do with his time, how was he going to keep himself amused? Seeing as every second of his life up until that point had been ruled by the Empire, he thought he might have to get some sort of a hobby.

The scaly alien need not have worried about what he was going to do once he was on Earth, since from the moment he'd left the battlestar his movements had been tracked by an X-wing fighter. As the shuttle touched the penumbra of the earth the shadowing rebel craft let loose with its cannons. The little ship took hit after hit and, mortally wounded, spun out of control. In a cloud of burning gases it fell through the air towards the night-time side of the blue-green planet.

In Spain there is no mention of Christmas holidays until mid-December but once they get going it can sometimes seem as if they are never going to end. The semi-official beginning is on the 22nd with the proclamation of *El Gordo* – the state lottery known as 'The Fat Boy'. The centrepiece is a five-hour TV show broadcast on the number-one channel, during which the winning numbers are called out by orphans from Madrid's San Ildefonso school. It's hard to believe that anywhere else in the world you could have a television spectacular that was just a handful of little orphaned boys chanting numbers into a microphone, but Bar Noche Azul was always crammed for the entire length of the programme.

Unlike in the UK the Spanish don't celebrate Christmas Day much. The night of the 24th is 'Noche Buena' – 'The Good Night' – traditionally the first big night of feasting and getting together with the family while the 25th is generally spent dozing around the house and picking at the remnants of the meal from the night before.

Even if the 25th had been more of a holiday, Stanley would still have been walking alone through the scrub-covered hillside high above the village, for one thing his mother wasn't the type to leave presents under the tree or invite the neighbours round for mulled wine. Last year they'd had their Christmas Day, complete with turkey and roast potatoes, presents, cards and a tree, on a Tuesday morning in the middle of July.

Stanley's mother Donna had lived in the village since she was a teenager. Roger her father had been one of the British pilgrim fathers, who had owned a little village house on Calle Carniceria for several years before even Laurence arrived. Nobody even knew he had a daughter, until suddenly sixteen-year-old Donna had turned up with a little baby in tow and announced she was going to make a new life for herself in Spain. According to Roger the father was a lonely Brazilian teenage footballer on an unsuccessful and bewildering three-month loan spell at Middlesbrough FC and that was why Stanley was half black. Roger said the footballer had been her first and she had only let him do it to her because she felt sorry for him.

The first time Laurence met Donna was in the local pharmacy. On entering he initially thought somebody had collapsed by the counter, perhaps after being diagnosed with some terrible disease but it was just the women who ran the shop fussing in a demented fashion over Donna's infant. Children in Spain were treated as visiting foreign potentates from repressive regimes were treated in Britain, traffic was stopped and work suspended. In the queue behind Donna people who needed vital medication understood that they were going to have to wait.

Laurence usually had great difficulty in talking to people much younger than himself, either he acted like he was some aged colonel who'd died at the time of the Crimean War or he had to stop himself speaking like an OG gangsta, saying 'whattup dawg?' and 'true dat' even if the kid he was talking to was a ten-year-old Chinese violin prodigy. Somehow with Donna, right from the start he always managed to just talk. Once he'd introduced himself she said, handing her child across the counter so that the shop assistants could really have a go, 'It would have been easy for me to have stayed in Darlington and finished my education you know? My mum was more than happy to look after Stanley or I could have kept him with me in the school's creche. I could have carried on going to clubs with my mates. All the other pregnant teenage girls on the estate shared out baby clothes they robbed from shops in town. Life was all right but it made me sick how the council would give every slut who got herself knocked up a nice little flat with two bedrooms and central heating. That's why I've come to Spain, to make something of myself. I'm a mother now, a lioness who must do anything to protect her cub.'

'Right . . .' Laurence said, '. . . and was the father really a Brazilian footballer?'

'Well, I don't know that he wasn't.'

As Stanley made his way across the rocky ground, icy wind slithering through the gnarled trees, his mind was filled with worry about his mother. She'd gone out last night and not come home; he would really have liked to go to Noche Azul just to check up that she was there and not injured and lying in a hospital somewhere, but he knew that if she was in the bar and he came around looking for her there was a good chance that she'd turn nasty.

So he figured it was best if he just went walking. But, unlike in the past, he found he couldn't leave his worry back down in the village, it came with him up into the mountains.

In many ways it was a good thing that in Spanish villages and towns, unlike in the UK, there was no separation between the young and old: they all used the same bars, went to the same fiestas, hung about in the same squares. In comparison, if you were to look at any town centre in Britain at night-time you'd think there'd been some sort of plague caused by an escaped virus, that had killed everybody over thirty while leaving the young survivors with terrible brain damage. Brain damage that caused them to reel about the streets vomiting, shouting, fighting and showing their breasts to passing policemen.

Still sometimes, if you were a kid in the village with a parent who was an abrasive, noisy person like Donna, then it would have been nice from time to time to get away from her, but it wasn't possible. You were stuck at a youth club where they let old people play on the ping-pong tables and dance at the disco.

At the moment for Stanley each new day seemed to bring some fresh and unpleasant thought or un-settling feeling. Yesterday it had been his confusion about the reasons why Simon hadn't come to meet him. Today Stanley was beginning to be concerned that a lot of people in the village thought of his mum as a bit of a nutter. Only two days before in Bar Noche Azul he'd seen her push past the owner Fabien to go and rummage in the kitchen fridge for some-thing to eat. Emerging with a chicken leg in her hand she'd said to her son, 'They love me in here', but the look on Fabien's face seemed a long way from love.

While Donna didn't seem to have any idea of how she was perceived, her son churned inside with embarrassment on her behalf. With an effort he decided that he couldn't cope right now with the worry of whether his mum was a figure of ridicule or not. He was probably getting everything back-wards. As he walked on, his agitation slowly decreased with each step he took away from the village. He'd been hiking for about three hours since he'd passed through the gate in the ancient walls, climbing steadily through the changing vegetation of the valley. Once past the orange and olive groves that surrounded his home, crossing streams and ancient water channels he travelled in the shade of oaks, maples and elms. Higher up still, Stanley emerged from the treeline onto rocky flatland, the windblown grass woven with creeping juniper and laburnum. Up on these slopes the shrubs were low, rosemary, thyme and lavender all flourished but never grew above about knee-high. In spring wild flowers in blues and purples would compete with the aston-ishing red of the poppies but right now the land-scape was almost monochrome. As he walked lizards scuttled away from his footfall towards the shelter of the dry brush.

Stanley paused for a second and surveyed the little clusters of habitation far below him that grew like white patches of pigment on the green skin of the mountains. Above him a griffin vulture wheeled lazily in the sky. Breathing heavily the boy clutched his thin jacket around him. Though the sky was an unremit-ting clear blue, even in the sunshine it was freezing.

Pressing on it took a while for him to notice that

a clump of Spanish firs towards which he'd been heading had been smashed apart by some large object which had left a path of still smouldering, scorched earth etched into the scrubland. Stanley paused and looked around for other human activity but there was only the shivering of grasses and the creaking of tree branches in the icy wind. Tentative at first he followed the trail of blackened soil which ran for nearly half a kilometre before it ended abruptly at a rocky outcrop against which something had smashed with tremendous force; the object now reduced to a few twisted ribs and melted clumps of some strange not quite metal-looking substance. The boy stared for a few seconds at the mangled wreck before noticing with a sudden start the body of a man lying face down in a cluster of broken cactus. Approaching closer his first thought was that the jacket of the man's dark suit, a bizarre sight in itself up here on the mountainside, had been torn open at the back and was standing proud of his carcass.

Initially Stanley assumed that he was looking at a murder victim. After all, in films people were always coming across murder victims. Sometimes these people became part of the plot but generally you never saw them again. It was one of the things he'd always worried about, finding a body. At school, when somebody committed a transgression and the teacher asked the class who'd done it, he inevitably had the compulsion to confess even though he was invariably innocent. He was convinced if he ever found a corpse he'd be unable to stop himself telling the Guardia Civil that he'd done it and knowing them they'd probably look no further but lock him up in the big prison near Cadiz with Runciman's dad. Only on closer inspection did he see, with enormous relief, that the thing wasn't a person and that the raised flap was in fact a door that opened into the body of whatever it was that was lying there. But what was this thing exactly, an unwanted figure from a waxwork museum of the last President of France but one? Or a shop window dummy from some old-fashioned haberdashers in Malaga's old town? Its neat dark suit certainly seemed pretty dated. But what was it doing up here?

Stanley knew that there was nothing the Spanish liked better than to come to a beauty spot and leave their rubbish, but this seemed a bit excessive even for them, especially since the nearest road was two hours' walk away and Spanish garbage leavers, not being fitness fanatics, always travelled by car or truck.

The boy took Valery Giscard d'Estaing, or whoever it was, by the ankles and tried to pull him out of the cactus, but either he was stuck or the dummy was incredibly heavy because he could not budge it even one centimetre. He paused for a minute, then skirting the spikes of the plant was able to edge himself alongside the prone form and peer inside. He now understood that it could be a costume of some kind and someone his size might find it possible to climb through the hatch and fit inside it.

Stanley suddenly thought of the large number of stray cats that lived in his village: they were fed, watered and their multiple medical needs attended to by a gang of middle-aged Englishwomen led by one called Miriam. Unlike the cats in other villages their coats were glossy, their eyes unclouded, clearly they didn't need to hunt for food, yet nearly every day there was some crisis amongst the women: a cat had got itself wedged down a drain or bricked up behind a wall or had fallen asleep in the boot of a tourist's car and now somehow had to be shipped back from Norway. Stanley, as he struggled unsuccessfully against the overwhelming desire to stick his head into the body of the prone figure, thought he now understood what drove the cats to get themselves stuck. Giving in to his irresistible curiosity he manoeuvred himself on top of the figure and slid his head inside. It felt cool and slightly rubbery against his skin, but not frightening, so he wriggled the rest of his body into the casing of the man, slipping his arms and legs within the arms and legs of the suit.

As soon as Stanley was completely enclosed all

the screens burst into life and the hatch door slammed shut. The boy was now trapped within the alien machine, pinioned into place by the close-fitting limbs. Immediately he panicked and tried to free himself. From the outside it appeared as if the man lying face down in the cactus had suddenly come to violent life, he began to writhe and twist on the ground, sending shards of plant and clumps of earth flying hundreds of metres in every direction with the ferocity and power of his movements. From inside the man's head there came an indistinct yelling.

After a minute of flailing the figure collapsed and lay still, then after a pause, and with great hesitation, the man began to climb unsteadily to his feet. Several times he pitched sideways back into the cactus but each time he slowly raised himself until eventually he stood swaying like a baby on unsteady legs. The big man in the suit remained motionless for some minutes, only his head pivoted from side to side, his strange black eyes seeming to take in the scene like a traffic camera, then he took a tentative step forward which sent him flying face down into the earth.

The whole process was repeated but this time the big man in the dark suit coped better, taking a number of wavering strides before he fell again.

With his head pressed into the inner skin of the

robot Stanley thought of how to open the suit. In his mind he imagined the back of it opening up and as soon as he did this the hatch at the rear of the robot unlocked, the door sprung open and a split second later Stanley came tumbling out of the back.

Slowly the young boy circled the huge, frozen figure of the man. 'Unbelievable!' he said to himself and then, just as the silly kitten re-enters the drain that has nearly cost it its life, Stanley climbed back into the machine. The door closed behind him and the man in the business suit climbed slowly to his feet, then set off back down the mountain, walking at first but after a while breaking into a joyful loping run. Swifter than the most sure-footed mountain goat he hurtled through the pink rock-rose and juniper towards the white village below, the muffled sound of whooping coming from inside his head.

The journey into the high country had taken the boy three hours but with the enhanced power of the suit he was able to return in something under thirty minutes. Soon he was back in cultivated land, travelling through orange groves and stone-walled terraces of almond trees.

When he got nearer to the steep Arabic walls of the village he paused then climbed down into a steep-sided *arroyo* – a river bed that was dry at this time of year but would become a torrent when the snows melted in spring on the high sierras. Crouching now the man ran along the gully until he came to a stone-walled shack called a *cortijo*, once used by a farmer but long since abandoned, which teetered on the bank above him. Scrambling up the sheer sides of the *arroyo* the man easily brushed aside the rotten wooden door of the shack and entered the building. In one corner the roof had collapsed onto the beaten earth floor so that it now formed a pile of termite-eaten logs and ancient brittle straw. The man in the suit effortlessly lifted the logs aside then went and stood in the dark corner of the *cortijo* facing its rough stone wall.

Abruptly all the rampant vitality went out of him and a few seconds later the door at the back of his body sprang open and Stanley climbed out. His plan had been to pile the logs against the robot but though the boy struggled mightily to shift them, he wasn't able to wrestle any of the wood back into place. Finally he gave up and contented himself with hiding the robot under a pile of straw, firewood, strips of dirty blue sacking and torn sheets of fibreboard.

Back at the crash site, hidden where he had fallen in the centre of a large patch of juniper, the body of the alien deserter lay. Buzzards descended and began to pick at the corpse, while tiny lizards scuttled from the nearby rocks and tore at him with their sharp teeth, then carried off small pieces of their fellow scaly creature to be devoured within the crevices of the mountain.

Navidad

Though it was Christmas morning Laurence was sitting at his usual table in Bar Noche Azul trying to read the copy of yesterday's *Guardian* that Stuart had brought out with him from England. An hour ago Stuart had gone back to Malaga in his little red Korean hire car and Laurence couldn't imagine he'd be coming back. Further down the valley the bars put out their own copies of the British papers, usually the *Guardian* or the *Independent* but it was thirty minutes' drive from here to a shop where you could buy the international press so he'd been anticipating sitting down with the paper and his breakfast before having to pass the increasingly tattered and greasy pages around the rest of the British community. Trouble was he found himself unable to concentrate on the stories of the people in the paper because he no longer knew who they were. His mind kept slipping off the stories saying this minister was doomed and that minister was on their way up, that this thing was a horror and this other thing was a delight and instead Laurence's thoughts continually slid back towards his breakfast. It was always the same thing, *pan tostada* – half a loaf smeared with a thin layer of mashed up tomato and garlic. That was all you could buy for breakfast in Noche Azul. He'd had a complicated relationship with *pan tostada*. For a while Laurence had loved *pan tostada* for its authenticity. Then after a few years he'd hated it, the same goddamn thing every day, it nearly drove him crazy. But then, about a decade in, there'd been a moment of surrender, of acceptance, like an alcoholic hitting their rock bottom, and he'd come to see the lack of choice as a good thing: his breakfast was something he couldn't change so now he loved it again. As far as breakfast went the lack of options was a liberation. Unfortunately, though he tried, Laurence didn't seem to be able to extend that surrender to the rest of his life. With an effort of will he forced himself to again stare at the pages of the newspaper blurred by his indifference. One column, written by a mad-looking Jewish guy, stated with complete authority that one thing would definitely happen, then beneath

it another column by a crazy-looking Muslim woman
said with the same authority that the complete opposite would happen.

Some change in the air made Laurence look up
from the paper. At first he didn't know what was
unsettling him then he saw that Donna's son Stanley
had come into the bar, presumably looking for his
mother. The boy was what Laurence's dear old mum
would have called 'half chat', and which he kept
having to remind her when she came out to visit was
now referred to as 'mixed race'. The boy's black curly
hair was hacked into a short afro that contrasted
oddly with his light caramel skin and the European
cast of his features. The face was dominated by big
brown eyes that to Laurence always seemed to be
pleading for something that nobody could give him.
Under his thin nylon jacket the boy wore a short-
sleeved white shirt that Laurence would have given
to a kid in a film who was good at chess and didn't
have many friends. On the boy's thin legs were too
short, ill-fitting jeans of cobweb-thin denim. Laurence
guessed that the whole lot had come from the budget
range at one of the hypermarkets on the Granada
ring road. For some reason they always gave these
cheapo brands names in mangled English such as
'basik's', 'Lord Mutley' or 'mister cheeZe', as if a
few words would give these trashy garments the
quality of Savile Row tailoring. Laurence was still

sometimes astounded at the shoddiness of the goods sold in Spanish stores compared to those in Britain: gardening tools that bent at the first stab at the soil, leaky hot water bottles that erupted during the night and clothes that looked like they were made from three-quarters dust. To dress your child in such tat amounted to child abuse in Laurence's book.

From where he sat he could see both Stanley and Donna. The boy's mother was in the small room at the back of the bar bent over the pool table. The position she was in gave him a good view of her boyish behind clothed in tight American jeans of a much better quality than her son's. They did not dress up much in the valley and she almost always wore these jeans along with tight T-shirts in pastel colours or washed out greys and blues that emphasised her slender frame. Her shoulder-length hair was the colour of pine furniture, her skin was much lighter than her son's and she had eyes of an unsettling, swimming-pool blue. She was now twenty-nine years old. Donna's movements were always quick, she laughed a lot, though not necessarily at anything funny and got really excited about a completely different thing every week, so that she was always organising outings to concerts in Cordoba, yoga classes or visits to reiki masseurs up in the Alpujarras.

Right now, sprawled provocatively over the table,

Donna was making laughing conversation with the two men she'd been playing pool with for the last couple of hours. Laurence finally acknowledged that this was the other thing that had been making him agitated. He really wasn't sure that the way she was behaving was such a good idea with those two; he had never seen these particular characters before but in this day and age the danger signals of Russian Mafia up from the coast were unmistakable.

During the Spanish civil war this had been an anarchist village, the black and red flag of the FAI – the *Federación Anarquista Ibérica* – had hung from the town hall roof for nearly three years and they held the regional record for shooting priests and nuns. Even if there was the most extreme kind of trouble the bar's owners Armando and his brother Fabien would never think of calling the Guardia Civil.

None the less Armando was clearly edgy at having the Russians in his bar and a few minutes before had called Fabien on the mobile to ask him to come downstairs from their flat above. The older brother, thinner and darker than his stocky sibling, had emerged holding the bat that he used once a year in the annual Spanish versus English village cricket match. Laurence guessed that Donna had been drinking with these two Russians since the night before and taking cocaine too, yet only she would be unaware, at least on the surface, of what all the other males in the bar – Armando, Fabien, Laurence, a few Spanish workers and now little Stanley – knew, that the two men she was with were trouble on a stick.

Laurence saw Donna's son hesitate, calculating the peril he was in, yet after a pause the boy still went up to his mother and pulling on her arm said, 'Mum, I've got something to show you, c'mon, it's really amazing . . .'

Donna turned and for a second incomprehension at why this little person was talking to her flashed across her face, before she suddenly seemed to realise that it was her son. It looked like she had set out the day before to forget for a short while that she was a woman with a child and had succeeded a bit too well.

'Not now Stan,' shaking him off, 'can't you see I'm celebrating Christmas with my friends Yuri and Sergei.'

'But Mum, I really want to show you this.'

'Show it me later, darlin',' she replied.

Petulantly Stanley said, 'You told me we didn't celebrate Christmas.'

'Well, I'm not sure if it is Christmas where these two come from.'

'That doesn't make sense.'

'You fuck off now kid,' said one Russian, stepping forward and slipping his hand underneath

Donna's T-shirt to caress her stomach while staring straight at the boy. 'We're havin' fun wit your Moms.'

Donna giggled nervously and pushed the Russian's hands away. 'Not in front of my son, Yuri.'

Laurence expected Stanley to back down at this point but something seemed to have made him less timid than usual.

'Leave my mum alone Yuri,' Stanley said.

'*Oh shit*,' Laurence thought, turning his gaze towards the counter where he could see that Armando was also straining under the quandary of what to do next. Laurence made a mental note that the British community really were going to have to have another attempt at doing something about Donna, she was making them all look bad.

The Russian paused for a second then stepped towards the boy and delivered a tremendous back-handed slap to the side of his face. 'Stop it!' Donna yelled as Armando and Fabien both came around the counter, only to be brought up short by the other Russian turning to them and pulling his jacket back to show the stubby little pistol tucked into his belt. Nobody knew what was going to happen next, only that chances were it was going to be bad.

Fortunately Stanley seemed to be the one who chose to act like a grown-up, taking one final look at the man who had slapped him he rushed out of the bar clutching the raw side of his face. Slowly the tension hissed out of the bar.

'Fucking kid,' Yuri said. Donna was crying now and the Russian turned his fury on her. 'Come on bitch, stop dat crying or I'll get mad now.' Snuffling, Donna pulled herself together.

'Sorry, Yuri,' she said. 'Kids, you know, they want too much attention.'

'Sure, whatever,' replied Yuri, losing interest. He called to Armando for more brandies and they returned to playing pool.

Laurence was hastily gobbling the last of his breakfast *tostada*, eager to get out of the bar and back to safety behind the high walls of his house. His mind told him he should have just abandoned everything when trouble first started, but here in the land of Lorca's 'Blood Wedding' there were certain notions of male honour that had to be adhered to even for him. If he'd just fled at the first sign of a fight and not eaten his breakfast he would have lost face with Fabien and Armando and, sadly, that was important to him.

'Too late . . .' Laurence said under his breath as the door of Noche Azul crashed open. Turning he saw framed against the wintry morning light a huge serious-looking man, his arms spread wide so that he seemed to fill the entire opening. The man wore a ridiculously neat suit, which to his eyes said United

States circa 1960, rather like something somebody in Frank Sinatra's entourage might have worn at the height of the Vegas Rat Pack years. Funny what you find yourself thinking when menace comes through the door, Laurence found himself thinking.

The strangest thing though, the chilling thing, as the man stood calmly looking around him, his head slowly swivelling from side to side, was that on his face, below the neat short swept-back black hair, there was no expression whatsoever, utter blankness. Laurence thought that he had never seen such emptiness on the face of a living being.

Though fuzzy with drink some ancient male radar had woken Yuri and Sergei to the fact that hazard had entered the bar. Yuri straightened and took the pool cue by its slender end while Sergei reached inside his jacket to grasp the pistol.

'Oh, Mother,' Laurence found himself incongruously whispering before the stranger, with three astonishingly quick strides, was upon the Russians. Sergei managed to get the pistol half out of his pants but the big man took his gun arm and snapped it with a simple twist, one shot rang out incredibly loud in the bar, the ejected cartridge case chinging onto the unyielding floor. Screaming with pain, Sergei did not get the chance to fire off another round as the big man lifted him with no apparent effort and threw the Russian one-handed against the back wall of the bar, cracking his skull on the lurid Spanish tiles, the blood that splayed onto their unyielding surface mingling with the jagged blues, yellows and reds.

The man turned to look for Yuri but he was long gone, out the front door down the street across the plaza by the church into his Mercedes onto the twisting road down the motorway and back to the coast.

Seeing that his prey had fled, the stranger's dead eyes alighted on the swaying figure of Donna. Wordlessly he walked towards her, took the woman gently by the arm and led her out of the bar. As they went she gave Armando, Fabien and Laurence a last beseeching look.

Noche Vieja

Back up in the black night of space, the Imperial cruiser had not, as the deserter expected, been destroyed. Though intensely battered she was still more or less in one piece, for at the climactic moment the rebel fighters had broken off their attack and fled in the direction of Saturn.

In his shattered command centre the captain of the ship took reports of the damage then called two subordinates to him. A pair of aliens scuttled into his presence. There's no sound on Earth that even approximates their names, the closest would be somebody trying to yodel with a mouthful of mice so we'll call the male Sid and the female Nancy. The captain said to the pair, 'At the height of the battle a shield operative abandoned his post, stole a Planetary

Exploration Suit and a shuttle craft and headed for the nearest planet. Possibly he was hit by an enemy fighter. We are not entirely certain because of the confusion of battle, but the monitor screens seem to show that he managed to land his ship on a particular sector of the planet below us.'

On the ship's screen a view of the earth appeared. The image zoomed in until it showed a section of Southern Spain, a red dot pulsing over the foothills of the Sierra Nevadas.

'He landed somewhere in this area, but at the moment, given the damage to our communications equipment, it isn't possible to be more accurate. The Imperial Navy will not allow desertion under any circumstances, and we cannot permit our technology to fall into the hands of the primitive creatures on that planet.'

As the captain talked two storage tubes similar to those from the Planetary Exploration Suit Room were brought in.

'I am sending you two down to the planet to bring back the deserter and to retrieve or destroy the suit. We do have two spare suits but they had to be brought out of deep storage. They are left over from our last visit about a hundred and fifty years ago.'

Sid and Nancy stared at the glass tubes. They were covered in thick dust so that it was impossible to see inside, at a signal from the captain the release switch of the first tube was pressed. Slowly and creakily the cylinder opened to reveal a frozen, immobile Victorian gentleman his face adorned with a splendid moustache and long sideburns. The man was dressed in a tall top hat and stiff tight grey suit and on his feet were shiny black patent leather boots. Then the other tube was opened to reveal his lady, as tall as the male. Golden curls spilled out from under her pink bonnet which framed a round, pretty, vacant face. A gigantic hooped skirt spread out from her slender waist above a tight green velvet jacket. Over her shoulder she daintily held a frilly parasol.

'These are your suits,' the captain said. 'Go down to the planet, locate the deserter, bring him and the suit back. You have thirty-six revolutions of the planet to complete your task. If you don't succeed, after that time we will be forced to destroy it.'

The man led Donna by the arm in a grip that was both gentle and unbreakable down the narrow alley of Calle Santo Segundo to the little house she lived in on the corner of Calle Carniceria. Into Donna's mind there suddenly popped a Lorca poem she'd heard a woman reciting at the checkout of the Carrefour supermarket in Granada. Andalucians are inclined towards declaiming bits of Lorca at almost any time – whether sitting on the bus, visiting the doctor or putting out a chemical fire at the docks.

The poem went:

I realised I had been murdered,
They searched cafés, cemeteries and churches,
They opened barrels and cupboards,
They plundered three skeletons to remove
their gold teeth,
They did not find me,
They never found me?
No, they never found me.

Now it was going to happen to her. She was about
to join the ranks of the village's disappeared.
Andalusia was a place where those drifting west-
wards, looking for opportunity sometimes reached
the end of their road. Somebody would turn up,
rent a house, say they were starting a business
providing eco pools or legal services, they would be
in Noche Azul every night shouting about how they
were half Chocktaw Indian or were hiding from the
Provisonal IRA, then one day they would be gone.
Inside the house a table might be turned on its side,
a window might be broken or shouting had been
heard in the middle of the night. The next day the
house would be let to somebody else. You got used
to these sudden absences and vanishings so it took
a while for Donna to notice that her own father had
disappeared. They had struggled on together in their
little house for four years, Donna, her baby and

Roger, who had tried hard to be some kind of father to them both but it was not in his nature.

One reason it took some time for her to realise he'd gone was that he took nothing with him and even left behind his car. Yet she did not inform the Guardia or organise a search party, since she had in her mind an idea of a vast row of little lightbulbs on a board with people's names above them and one day a person's fizzled and went out, but right now she thought Roger's light still burned.

As the big man steered her down the moonlit streets Donna realised that all this time she might have been lying to herself and her father could have been disappeared just as surely as she was going to be. He had certainly made enough enemies, from his various schemes, rackets and scams. Maybe Roger was buried in the orange grove alongside the village's other troublesome corpses. Maybe he'd been killed and his body driven in the trunk of a car to be disposed of under the concrete of some raw new shopping mall east of Malaga – apparently 25 per cent of the foundations of some of those places was composed of corpse. Then she thought, what would happen to her son? Donna wondered what a Spanish orphanage was like, they probably gave the kids wine for lunch. She supposed if he was lucky he might get to announce the Christmas lottery numbers on the TV.

Next a wave of anger at the stupidity she'd shown overwhelmed her. She would never get to present her own property-developing TV show now, or build her own gated community – all of her plans were never going to happen. Instead this huge man, some disgruntled associate of the Russians probably, was going to torture her for information she didn't have, then strangle her. She'd told herself that Yuri and Sergei were just a couple of guys to have fun with but she must have known all along what they were like, it was as if there were two Donnas who didn't talk to each other: one who got chatting with dangerous men and the other who pretended that nothing was ever going to go wrong, no matter how crazy things got. Now that attitude was going to get her killed.

She unlocked the front door with shaking hands and they stepped into the dark living room, which suddenly felt much too small. The man's head actually brushed the black beams of the ceiling, but surprisingly he did at least release her. Donna eased out of his grip and not knowing what else to do switched a light on, except that as the power was still out nothing happened. 'Can I, erm, get you a coffee or something,' she said to the silent, shadowy stranger. This phrase seemed to be some kind of spell or hypnotic suggestion because as soon as she said it all life went out of him. She had never seen such lack of animation in a person, not even a dead one: her Gran lying in a coffin in the front room in Darlington had seemed more alive than this fellow. The man was standing there but you could tell that there was no spirit to him, he was as frozen as a squid on the seafood display at the Carrefour supermarket.

Then as if that wasn't enough weirdness for one Christmas Day, all the lights came on and at the same time her son appeared, jumping out of mid-air from behind the stranger.

'Hello, Mum,' he said popping his head around the frozen man.

'Stanley?' she said, then in a sudden rush of panic shouted, 'Stan! Get away from that man, quick! He's dangerous, he smashed up Sergei. I think I put him into a coma or something by asking him if he wanted a coffee but he might come round at any second . . .'

Of course kids never did what you wanted them to do even when there was terrible danger and amazingly Stanley just laughed at her warning. She would have slapped him except she was afraid to go anywhere near the man. Next, even more stupidly, he put his little hand on the enormous arm of the frozen figure.

'No, Mum,' he said, 'you don't understand. He can't come to life; he was me, I was him, I was inside him. He can't come round without me being inside him.'

This was all too messed up. 'Look,' Donna said in a voice as calm as she could muster, 'I'm going to go and phone the Guardia, no maybe not that. I'm going to go and get the car and we can drive to the coast or up into the mountains and we'll stay there for a few days and when we get back I expect this man will be gone.'

It felt really weird to Donna to be having this conversation while the guy was standing there like some totem pole. Even though he'd wanted to do her over, and God knows what else, it still felt like she was being somehow rude to him. All her life she had squashed herself in the company of men, listened to their idiotic opinions, stayed more or less faithful to them until they got out of prison and right now it didn't seem nice to be talking so brazenly in front of such a big, tough-looking one.

Still her son wouldn't shift, continuing to talk to her in the patronising tone of voice she recognised that kids used to describe the intricacies of the latest bizarre Japanese gadget they're obsessed with: a clam but also a rocket that's also a high-school kid who's saving the world from another more evil clam. Rocket, high-school kid, evil clam, Donna realised her brain was in danger of overheating.

Fortunately Stanley said in a calm voice, 'No, Mum, honest, he's harmless. Come and look round at the back of him.'

His gestures seemed so certain that with an un-
confident shuffle Donna edged round the rigid figure
until she was behind it. What she saw there nearly
stripped the gears of her already frazzled mind.

'Stanley. What the . . . ? I mean how? I mean what
the . . . ?'

Now that she could see it for herself Stanley talked
in a happy babble. 'I found it . . . I found it in the
high country. There was like a crash fire, something
from the sky had come down and burned and he
was lying next to it with his back open. So I got in
and he came to life. He's sort of like a Terminator
but also you can wear him like a suit of armour and
there's these screens inside that show where you're
going and other stuff I haven't figured out yet . . .'

Donna circled the robot tentatively touching it
and peering inside.

'But . . . where did it come from?'

'Outer space of course.' Stanley said this with the
certainty of someone for whom computer-animated
figures on TV were as real as the village baker.

'Outer space. I don't think so. How do you know
it isn't it like some sort of secret military thing?'

Stanley snorted. Donna thought it was amazing
how supercilious somebody who didn't know
anything about life could be.

'What, the Spanish military? Don't be dense,
Mum. They don't even have modern hats, never

mind gear like this. No,' he said with unassailable confidence, 'this is from outer space, no question. It's sort of like a space suit, but one that lets them explore earth without being detected. And it's strong as well. Mum, I can smash down trees and jump really high and run really fast. It's incredible, Mum.'

'Won't they be looking for it then, the space people?' Donna asked.

Her son thought about this for a second. 'Well, no, I don't think so. The alien that was in it wasn't around. There'd been a big fire and I think it was his spaceship that got burned. I reckon he was hurt and staggered off somewhere. So I don't know but I don't think so.'

Absentmindedly Donna said, 'You shouldn't have done that to Sergei and Yuri.'

'He hit me, Mum.'

'Yeah, I suppose Yuri was in the wrong too.' Then sticking her head inside the body of the Exploration Suit she said.

'Blimey. It's amazing. And only somebody exactly your size could fit into it?'

'Yeah. I guess so.'

Donna brightened, the sudden lifting of danger always made her euphoric, indeed in her few quiet moments she sometimes wondered if that was why she got into so many scrapes. 'Let's go back to the bar, me, you and that thing,' she said.

'What?'

'Let's go back to the bar in a while, first I'll have a little siesta then a bath and change my clothes and stuff then we'll go back. After all, the last time everybody saw us, him over there was dragging me out through the door to do God knows what to me. They'll be worried about my safety.'

Stanley thought that if they'd been so worried about her safety they would have come round to see if everything was all right by now but he didn't say anything.

His mother paused on her way to the bathroom and said, 'We should give him a name.'

'A name. Why?'

'I'll have to introduce him to people, stupid.'

'But he can't talk.'

'Well, I'll tell them he can't talk but he still needs a name.'

Stanley, annoyed that his mum seemed to be taking over his find, tried to get back some of the initiative by saying, 'We could call him Mister Robot.'

Donna said, 'No, don't be thick – not Mister Robot, that would give the game away, don't you think? Use your brain Stanley! Anyway, nobody's called Mister Robot.'

Stanley tried to think through the sudden fog of irritation that he felt towards his mum. It was always like this, they'd be talking quite naturally, then out of the blue she'd turn nasty. 'Mister Roberts!' he shouted. 'That's what we'll call him! We'll call him Mister Roberts.'

Donna tried it on for size. 'Mister Roberts . . . Mister Roberts. Laurence, Armando, Fabien, meet my new boyfriend Mister Roberts.'

'Your what?'

Sid and Nancy climbed into their Planetary Exploration Suits and travelled in them to the shuttle craft bay, taking a route almost identical to the one the deserter had employed. All over the ship, crew members were frantically repairing wreckage caused by the battle.

Waiting for them at the bay was a craft similar to the one the escaped alien had stolen. Because of damage from the fighting it had not been possible to provide them with many sophisticated tracking devices to hunt their quarry or anything particularly advanced to enable them to survive on the alien planet; the last thing the captain had told them was that their shuttle craft only had food supplies for a couple of days, but once the damage from the fighting had been sorted out their rations would be replenished from the mother ship.

The Victorian couple strode on board the craft and sat down on a bench at the back of the cockpit, the couple then climbed out of the rear hatches and settled themselves in the pilot and co-pilot seats in front of the control panel. They strapped themselves in, then Sid set a course for the blue-green planet below them, his partner took control and steered the little ship out of the docking port and into the silence of infinite space. For a few seconds the shuttle craft drifted beside the hull of the battlestar, then the main drive engaged and they sped away from the battered hulk towards the Earth's atmosphere. In the cockpit the sight of the silent pair in their antique clothes seated behind the two aliens with the reptilian skin had the appearance of the young Prince Albert and Queen Victoria being taken for a drive by two escapees from the zoo.

'Look!' Nancy said, pointing at the radar screen of the little shuttle craft: it was filled with the image of a thousand pulsating dots that swarmed around the Imperial Battlestar. As quickly as they'd gone the rebel fighters had returned.

You knew you had been in Bar Noche Azul too long when the sausages came round again. Here in the High Sierras tapas was still a gift given free to those who bought only the simplest drinks of wine and beer, the food cooked by the wives and mothers of the bars' owners. Those who came into the bar for a drink when it opened at 7 a.m. had little saucers of *piquillo al cabales* – peppers stuffed with Spanish blue cheese – plonked down in front of them, *ensaladilla russa* followed, then *morcilla*, the black pudding made by Fabien and Armando's mum and, in a more profound way, by the pig Armando kept tethered out the back of the bar, the pig which would be slaughtered every year at the Matanza, the day just after the new year when all the local pigs were killed and the streets ran red with blood. Manchego cheese and *membrillo*, a quince jelly from the Asturias appeared at around twelve noon, following that came prawns *a la Plancha*, then *buñuelos de espinacas*, tiny spinach fritters, then the bar's own chorizo, a particularly spicy sausage made by Fabien and Armando's mum and the pig. Next there was *jamón de Trevélez*, thin slices of snow-cured ham on chunks of rough local bread and finally goat's cheese preserved in oil from the Alpujarras. Approximately eight hours later the *piquillos al cabales* came back, and the whole process began again. Laurence sat at a table staring woozily at four plates of chorizo piled in front of him. He couldn't figure it out: according to the tapas on the table he had been in Noche Azul for nearly two days, that couldn't be right – he was certain he'd spent last night at home with Stuart. Laurence concluded it was wrong to try and tell the time with sausages.

He had desperately wanted to run home after

Donna had been dragged out of the bar by the big silent man, but as usual she left chaos behind that needed clearing up, namely Sergei lying passed out and bleeding on the floor. Armando and Fabien had decided this was a problem for the English to deal with so he'd had to call on his neighbour Baz and Baz's pickup truck. Baz was builder to the British and one of the original community who'd been living in the valley since the late eighties; when something physical needed doing he was the automatic choice.

Laurence phoned and explained what had happened; at first Baz thought Laurence was exaggerating but a couple of his Spanish labourers who'd been in the bar confirmed the tale of the giant man in the suit. A few minutes later he rolled up and with the labourers' help Sergei was loaded in the back of the pickup and covered with a tarpaulin. Then they drove down the valley and along the old road, where they were less likely to encounter a Guardia checkpoint, to the town of Durcal where Baz and the labourers dumped Sergei in a chair in the reception of the twenty-four-hour clinic. When they returned they said the Russian's breathing had become very shallow, but that wasn't their problem anymore.

Afterwards they'd all needed a drink to calm their nerves and then the rest of the British had started to drift into the bar and they'd had to be brought up to speed on what had happened so that now it had turned into yet another lost afternoon in Noche Azul.

Seated around a long table was almost the entire British community, *La Comunidad Ingles* as the locals called them. There was Nige, a tall dark-haired woman of forty, who everybody considered very beautiful, especially in comparison to the squat brown Spanish women. She was a sculptor with a big studio space and living quarters in a rambling four-storey house right at the very centre of the village in the small plaza where Calle Carniceria and Calle Trinidad met. Nige's dogs Dexter and Del Boy, two big matching yellow things lay outside on the bar's terrace. Next to her was Frank, a middle-aged Londoner who had foolishly let himself be persuaded by TV property programmes that he could make his fortune renovating a house in the village and had spent every penny of his redundancy on it. He worked on the house each day and the more effort he put into it the more decrepit it seemed to become. Alongside Frank was Kirsten, who was Dutch, which more or less made her an honorary Brit, except her spoken English was much more precise and erudite than theirs. She was an academic who worked for the European Community in Brussels on matters of social compliance, but since she spent most of her time in the village they didn't appear to miss her. To Kirsten's right was Li Tang, a Singaporean woman who owned a big walled house on the edge of the village and who was always extremely vague about her activities. Opposite Laurence was Janet a retired BBC executive, who lived in a small house facing Nige's. She had a small pension and a small dog who was also called Janet (or more usually 'Little Janet'). At the other end of the table was Baz, next to him was Miriam from Macclesfield who owned a farmhouse hidden in the woods below the village walls. She'd taken early retirement from the Solihull planning department on mental health grounds, having instituted a one-way system in the centre of town where all the roads went in different directions, some of them vertical. Her three-legged black mongrel called Coffee Table sat squirming nervously beside her. Both Janet and Miriam had more than one dog, in fact they each had about five back at their houses or dotted around the streets, in addition to numerous cats that they fed but Armando and Fabien rigidly enforced a one dog per customer rule in the bar.

Lastly there was Leonard, a writer of feminist science fiction of impenetrable obscurity, all about planets populated entirely by big red-headed women. Like Laurence, Leonard had one of the bigger houses in the village, hidden behind an anonymous white wall and reached via a tiny studded gate.

Laurence glanced towards the entrance where with an electric little skip of his heart he saw Donna and the enormous shape of a man standing in the doorway. As the couple walked towards the bar Donna linked her arm in that of the man's. 'This is nice,' she said in a loud voice.

The dogs lying on the ground stirred and began growling through clenched teeth in a strange high-pitched fashion that their owners had never heard before as Donna and the huge man, a tile snapping under his heel, crossed the floor.

Armando took hold of the cricket bat lying under the counter and several of Baz's Spanish workers who'd been drinking at the bar straightened and reached behind them for the big folding knives they carried tucked in the back pockets of their pants.

The British were overcome with a collective feeling of shiftiness. None of them had thought to check on Donna after she'd been dragged out of Noche Azul but then they reminded themselves Donna was the sort of girl that that sort of thing happened to. Anyway, the Brits reasoned she now seemed to be best friends with her attacker so they'd been wise to do nothing.

Donna and the man strode confidently over to the foreigners' table and sat down at a couple of spare seats. Donna beamed at everyone. 'So, who's going to get me a drink?' she asked.

Baz was the first to respond. 'Yeah sure, what do you want?'

'Rum and coke.'

'And your friend?'

'Oh he doesn't drink,' Donna said.

'A water or fruit juice or something?'

'No he doesn't drink like . . . anything.'

Baz couldn't really see how this could be but still he said, 'Right, OK.'

'So, hello everybody,' Donna said, 'this is my new friend Mister Roberts. He erm . . . he can't speak but he can hear. So you can, you know, you can say hello to him.'

'Doesn't he have a first name?' asked Janet.

'Yeah, probably . . .' Donna replied, 'but he can't tell me what it is can he?'

'No, I suppose not,' Janet replied confused.

Everybody said hello to Mister Roberts.

'Hello, Mister Roberts.'

'Hello, Mister Roberts.'

'Hola, Señor Roverts.'

'Hello there, Mister Roberts.'

There then followed a silence as the arrival of this huge, hulking inscrutable man cast a pall over the little group.

Janet leant across and whispered into Donna's ear 'So why can't he talk?'

Donna mouthed back 'throat cancer', and pulled a face suggestive of great suffering.

'Poor man,' said Miriam, peering at the vibrant giant. 'He looks well on it, though.'

'Positive visualisations.'

Laurence said, 'None the worse for your experiences of this morning, I see.'

'No indeed,' Donna preened. 'Haven't you ever had men fighting over you, Laurence?'

'People in the entertainment business don't fight with each other, dear, that's far too healthy and civilised compared with what they get up to. Anyway, that wasn't a fight, it was a beating up. Poor Sergei, we thought he was dead and we'd have to bury him in the same place where we . . .'

'But he was still breathing,' Miriam said, jumping in because he was coming up to very dangerous ground here. 'So Baz put him in the back of his pickup truck and he dumped your friend in the waiting room of the clinic in Durcal. If you were thinking of sending flowers or anything.'

With a frown, Nige, who never drank as much as the rest of them, asked, 'Donna, where's Stanley? From what I heard he seemed a bit freaked out by everything, is he OK?'

Donna gave a silly little smile. 'Oh, he's fine, he's nearby. Don't worry about Stanley.'

With a sudden crack Mister Roberts' chair, unable to sustain his great weight, buckled under him and he fell to the ground. The big man lay on the prawn-shell-strewn floor staring up at them with his blank face.

La Comunidad Ingles would talk about that Christmas Day in Bar Noche Azul for months to come. Sometimes, very occasionally, it happened that an evening caught fire like this and the plain bar with its lurid colour scheme and twenty-year-old posters, an ordinary room with a snooker table and fruit machine, the same freezing cold space where they saw each other day in and day out, where they ate their breakfast and their lunch, seemed suddenly transformed into a glittering ballroom filled with the sexiest, wittiest and most erudite personalities in the whole of Europe. Laurence supposed all the drink and drugs had a lot to do with the transformation. Yet on this occasion they weren't that important, rather it was the silent looming presence of Mister Roberts that seemed to bring everyone to a pitch of hysterical excitement. From time to time one of them would try to talk to him, address some remark, ask how long he'd been in Spain or whether he wanted to take care of a stray dog but he would just stare expressionlessly with his strange dark brown eyes, eyes that seemed as if they looked straight through them, directly into their souls. That sensation stirred them on to drink more alcohol and shout more nonsense and feel each other up as if Mister Roberts was some kind of maypole around which they danced their springtime fertility dance.

To Laurence the night resembled the DVD of a strange foreign film that had its subtitles missing and which some controlling entity was playing on fast forward, everyone in the bar was all flailing arms and jabbering mouths. Suddenly there would be a brief moment when the entity hit the pause button and he would see the crowd around him all frozen in mid yelp. In one of these brief moments of clarity it struck him with a stab of loneliness that nearly everybody in the bar had made money out of him at one time or another. For a start, he was certain that Nige had sold him his house for considerably more than she'd paid its original Spanish owners. Baz had done the building work to expand the house and to install the swimming pool and that had cost him a fair chunk of change, then for a while Miriam had charged him a fortune to plant and maintain his garden, until she got the idea that some of the plants were talking about her behind her back. And then, of course, there was Donna.

There existed a hierarchy in the village which had nothing to do with class or wealth, rather it concerned how much time you spent in the place. Those who lived in the village permanently were united in mild contempt for the Brits who owned second homes in the valley, and the ones who owned second homes looked down on those here on holiday who only rented. Donna attempted to make a living from all three groups. She rented out a little village house that she'd bought and done up when prices were low, she went in for a bit of property developing, buying and selling tiny scraps of land with highly suspect planning permissions, she did some translation work, she cleaned pools and she looked after other people's houses while they were back in the UK.

Laurence, back when she had sometimes called herself his personal assistant, when he and Donna had been good friends and they were having one of their late-night talks curled up on his sofa, said, 'Don't you think your taste for all these dangerous men – all the Brit hard cases from the coast, the Spaniards, the gypsies both single and married, that German transvestite who beat you up and ruined your tights – don't you think it's all an attempt to capture the wild youth that you think has been stolen from you by having a child so young, and by you having to make your way in the world without any help?'

Her face hardened, clearly intimating to Laurence that she didn't want to go into the subject. Laurence knew that sometimes you could say all kinds of things to Donna, get her to admit to all sorts of personality defects (though she never attempted to change any of them) while on other occasions she got very hostile if you suggested even the smallest flaw. 'Oh yeah?' she asked, 'and where did you do your degree in psychology, Doctor Laurence?'

'Pinewood University, dear,' he replied, frightened of offending her and so allowing himself to be derailed, 'that's where I studied. When you work in the movie business, with directors and producers and actors and, my God!, actresses, you learn all you need to know about the human mind because everybody experiences everything in bigger portions than the ordinary mortal. They feel they have to undergo every human emotion but they must do it forty times larger than anybody else so they fill up the silver screen.'

'Sounds exhausting,' she had replied. 'You're better out of it. You should be glad you don't get much work anymore.'

In the end, he reflected, his sensitivity hadn't made any difference, Donna had fallen out with him anyway.

*　　*　　*

It was well into Boxing Day morning before Donna and her companion were back through the door of their house and into the kitchen. Mister Roberts went limp and lifeless and after a few seconds Stanley climbed out of his back.

'Aw . . .' said Donna, approaching the silent machine. 'I was hoping for a dance.'

She went closer and began running her fingers tipsily across the face of the robot.

'Mum, leave him alone,' Stanley said over his shoulder as he rummaged in the fridge looking for something to eat. Finding some leathery chorizo at the back of the frost-furred shelves he put the meat in his mouth and chewed. They were both staring at the big silent man when Donna said:

'You know, Stan, how people are always letting me down?'

Her son nodded, it was a story that was repeated time and time again in their lives like a plotline from a long-running sitcom. When his mum made a new friend it was like she was falling in love. She always became friends with her new friend's friends, got tangled up in their lives and Stanley would reluctantly become close with the new friend's kids, even if he didn't like them that much. But as his mum said, the thing was they were never really grateful enough. There she was running around, picking them up from the airport or cleaning their poxy house, so why shouldn't she take a few sheets from their bed just to furnish her holiday let or why couldn't she have a swim or throw the odd party in their garden, seeing as they only used their stinking house about four weeks a year? Even then, when the arguments started, she'd try and keep everything nice and polite but the people always forced some kind of bust up and then he couldn't mix with their kids anymore because his mum would get really upset if she saw him with them.

'But Mister Roberts here,' Donna said in a quiet voice, 'he'll never let me down will he Stan? And he's big and strong, I bet there's things he could do . . . well we don't know yet do we? There's got to be all kinds of possibilities.'

After a pause in a different voice she said, 'Stanley?'

'Yes, Mum?'

'I was wondering. Have you looked at him closely, is there like a man's body under there, do his clothes come off and stuff?'

'No,' Stanley replied his voice muffled, still chewing on the ancient chorizo, 'I've looked and he's all one piece of a sort of plasticky metal.'

'Oh well,' Donna said, 'that's good I suppose. Easy to keep clean with a damp cloth.'

*   *   *

Later on that Boxing Day Donna woke from sleep with, for once, no hangover. She made herself a cup of coffee and putting on a warm coat went up onto the roof terrace, from there she breathed in her favourite view of the snow-tipped mountains that encircled the little cluster of houses. Turning she studied the valley and the ravine on whose edge the village teetered. Supposedly in Arabic the name of the valley was 'The Valley of Happiness', usually Donna thought 'Valley of Drunkenness' might be a better description but this afternoon, looking out at the bright blue sky, the deep red hillsides, the dark green citrus groves, their trees heavy with fruit she felt she might be able to agree with the original name. Donna was feeling unusually optimistic because she had an idea of what Mister Roberts' first task might be.

It was like she'd wished on a star and her entreaty had come true. A man had arrived who could protect her, who would be a friend and an ally, who would make people fear and respect her and would never leave her. When you thought about it it was a proper Christmas miracle.

One of the village houses Donna looked after was owned by a retired couple from Swansea. About a year ago they'd emailed her to say that because of illness they wouldn't be using it for holidays in the near future and they asked that she advertise it as being for rent, this she did in various British newspapers and on her website.

Donna finally managed to let the house to a potter named Monty Crisp and his girlfriend. He was in his late fifties, bald with a ponytail and muscular in a stringy, sinewy sort of way. He always wore baggy faded T-shirts and loose-fitting cotton trousers in gaudy prints, such as weightlifters wore on their days off. His girlfriend Dawn still dressed like the model she'd been in the sixties though her skin was now wrinkled and scored like the hide of a rhinoceros. Donna had let them have the house at a low rent because they'd told her that they were looking to buy a ruin or a plot of land on which they intended to build a big house of their own and they wanted her to find it for them. Figuring that she would be able to charge Monty and Dawn a huge commission on the sale, for three months Donna drove the couple from house to house, took them to dinner and listened to their endless stories about their circle of friends who all seemed to be the second division, provincial versions of famous personalities. 'He was the Humphrey Lyttleton of Derby' they would say of some bore they hung around with or 'they were the Ted Hughes and Sylvia Plath of Luton' which was their way of describing a pair of librarians they'd met on holiday in Crete. Of course Donna didn't know who the originals were of any of these people but she diligently looked them up afterwards on

Google. Still, she was confused by somebody Monty and Dawn described as the 'Graham Greene of Berkhamsted' once she discovered that the real Graham Greene came from Berkhamsted.

After three months and all the work she put in, the couple abruptly stopped paying rent on the house citing a long list of non-existent faults and refusing to move out until these non-existent faults were rectified. It drove Donna crazy that she had been played by these wizened old chancers but when she cut off their water and electricity they denounced her to the Guardia Civil. Because tenants' rights are very strong in Spain and because the Guardia were always happy to inconvenience one of the *Comunidad Ingles* they forced her to restore the services, which made Donna even more crazy.

The day after Boxing Day and Monty Crisp lay sprawled across the cheap and grimy plastic sun lounger on his roof terrace basking in the warm winter sun and revelling in the same view over the mountains, thinking that it was about time he re-henna'd his thinning hair and ponytail.

Suddenly there was a ferocious pounding on the front door, Monty levered himself up from the lounger and peered over the parapet. Looking down he saw a familiar sight – the top of Donna's angry head. Beside her stood a dark-haired man.

Monty smiled to himself, the door was made of sturdy Spanish oak; its solid iron bolts had survived attacks from the Moors, Visigoths, Falangists and Donna running her four-wheel drive into it.

He stepped back from the parapet. Since they'd stopped paying rent Monty and Dawn always made sure they never went out of the house together – this morning his partner had slipped out at 5 a.m. to drive to the hippy market in Orgiva where she had a stall selling fusewire butterflies of her own creation. As long as one of them was on the premises any forced reclamation would be illegal.

The potter's confident smile faded a little as he heard a tearing sound and again peering into the street saw that the big man had somehow torn the door from its hinges and was now in the process of stacking it neatly against the wall of the house opposite. Next he saw the pair enter his house.

Rushing downstairs Monty found Donna and her companion standing calmly in the living room waiting for him. Seen from ground level the man was much, much bigger than he'd appeared from above. None the less, Monty's ponytail bobbing about with righteous indignation at the invasion of his home, the older man shouted, 'What do you think you're doing? You're going to have to pay for that door!' and reaching for his mobile phone said, 'I'm phoning the Guardia about this right now!'

Quite gently the big man reached across, took the phone out of Monty's hand and crushed it as if it were made from balsa wood and silver paper.

'Now, Monty,' Donna said. 'You've had a good run, but you really need to pay your back rent for the last six months. Of course, you could denounce my friend Mister Roberts here to the Guards, after all it was him that did all the damage, but Monty, I want you to look deep into Mister Roberts' eyes and I want you to tell me if you really feel like upsetting a man with eyes like that.'

Trembling, but unable to stop himself Monty looked up from the wreckage of his ancient Nokia scattered on the tiled floor and stared hypnotised into the dark orbs of Mister Roberts. He'd never witnessed such blankness in the gaze of another human being. Yet there was still some core of stubbornness or ingrained meanness in the old hippy which made him gasp out. 'No, you're not getting anything out of me . . .'

'Oh, Monty, Monty, Monty,' Donna said with a vicious little smile on her face. 'You are not going to like what happens next.'

Late that evening when Dawn got back from Orgiva in their old post office van she almost drove past Monty sitting hunched up and trembling in front of the town hall with all their belongings heaped around him and a terrified look in his eyes. She stopped in the middle of the square and hurriedly clambered out of the driver's seat. 'Monty, for heaven's sake, what's wrong, what's happened?' she asked the quaking figure clutching its knees and whimpering on the cold stone steps.

It took Monty a good fifteen seconds to haul himself back from whatever terrible place he was in. 'That's the last time we rent a cottage from the *Guardian*,' was all he said.

Across from Noche Azul was the village's basketball court which, like most of the improvements in the last few years, had been paid for by a generous grant from the EC. In the bar when the locals started their usual moaning about the perfidious *Ingles* hanging on to Gibraltar, Baz would shout back at them, 'You can 'ave the rock back when you give me back all the bleeding Sports Halls, Highways and regional parliaments my UK taxes have paid for!'

All the Brits knew that Baz had never actually paid any tax when he'd been in the UK, which was one of the reasons why he'd had to move to Spain, but they agreed with his general point.

The concrete, mosaic inlaid bench in the shape of an angel in front of the court was where the teenage boys and girls gathered after school. Overlooking this scene seated at their usual table on the terrace of Noche Azul, faces upturned to the bright winter sun but bodies wrapped in down-filled ski jackets, Laurence said to Nige, 'Have you noticed how the young Spanish girls have changed over the last few years? A while back seeing them come off the school bus they were these stubby-legged, black-haired peasant girls, bodies perfectly suited for farm work. Now there's all these willowy things with blond highlights and tight trousers showing off their flat brown bellies. These girls look like five minutes working in the fields would kill them.'

'It'd certainly make a mess of their nails,' Nige said.

Laurence sighed. 'Sometimes, you know, I miss the way things were when I first came here. When there were donkeys in the streets and you and me, Roger and Baz were the only Brits.'

'Well, things change, Laurence, and you can't stop them and we're not doing such a bad job of holding on to a lot of the old ways up here. Besides, your old mate Donna's been doing her bit to scare away any more British coming here with her new friend Mister Roberts.'

'You heard about yesterday then?'

'Miriam told me Monty had to be sedated with some of her nervous breakdown pills before they could get him into their van to take him to Granada Airport. If Monty Crisp goes around telling the

Frida Kahlo of Basingstoke and the Pablo Neruda of Darlington what happened and it puts them off coming to the valley, then it's no bad thing.'

'Sure,' Laurence said, 'but I was there with Miriam, I saw Monty before he went and the look on his face and the things he said Donna got Mister Roberts to do to him . . .'

'Oh, I expect he's just exaggerating because he got scared out of the house that he was living in for free.'

Laurence didn't feel able to let it go. 'I'm not sure if I don't believe what he said. You don't know Donna like I do, that girl is full of fury. It's not a good idea for any of us if she has a sidekick like Mister Roberts, somebody who seems happy to do what she wants. She's not that stable in the first place.'

'Oh, Laurence, you always get like this with women you used to be friends with. And if it comes to it, well, we've dealt with difficult women before.'

'I know, but I'll tell you something, you haven't been in the middle of this like I have. You weren't there when Mister Roberts messed up Sergei. I bet if you'd seen the power of that man you'd feel differently. And another thing, Sergei got a shot off and his gun was pointing directly at Mister Roberts, but the man didn't react in any way.'

'Well, the bullet must have gone somewhere else.'

'Darling, I've looked all over Noche Azul but I haven't found the hole if it did.'

'Oh, is that why you were crawling around the bar on your hands and knees last night?'

'No, that was just drunkenness, drunkenness and despair, you know, the usual.'

'So are you saying bullets can't harm Mister Roberts, that he's immortal or a zombie or something?'

'I don't know what I'm saying apart from the fact that him and her together is a dangerous combination.'

After a few more minutes of contemplative basking Laurence said to Nige, 'You know, I've always been suspicious of people who act as if they know exactly and in minute detail what was going through the mind of their childhood selves. As if the person they were at the age of ten or whatever is on the other end of the phone or easily reachable by email, like they could just call them up and say, "Hi, Childhood Self, now just remind me why were we so desperate to take our pet snake along to our first day of secondary school?"

'For me, young Laurence disappeared when he was about twenty, leaving no forwarding address. After that age I can more or less dimly figure out why I did what I did but before then I haven't the faintest idea what was going through my head. I can only guess at why my favourite books at the age of eight were the novels of Graham Greene or the reason why I was a supporter of Cardiff City football club even though I'd never been to Wales or why I wanted a javelin and a rolling pin for my ninth birthday. That's not to say that I didn't go through inner turmoil, after all something must have formed my personality. It's just that the emotional memory of my formative years is a complete blank, as if the computer file has been wiped by a wild power surge on some forgotten, stormy night.'

Nige said, 'I think that might just be you. I can remember lots about my childhood, too much really, the number of my Aha fan-club membership and an entire episode of the *Bionic Man*. It's yesterday and today I struggle with.'

'I was just thinking about young Stanley. I'm fond of that boy, but since I fell out with Donna she won't let me have anything to do with him; I can't say I was the best man to have in his life but I've got to be better than that Mister Roberts.'

'You were the closest thing to a mother that he ever had.'

'You know, I say I remember nothing of my childhood, but funnily enough one thing which is quite vivid is that point when you start to see all adults, especially your parents, not as the godlike figures they were to you when you were an infant but as real, fallible people. For me it happened when I was on the bus to school and the conductor forgot to take my fare. Up until that point I thought grown-ups knew everything, that there was a daily newsletter or something that said "little Laurence is going to try and not pay his fare today". Once I realised they didn't know any more than me it made the world seem a lot more dangerous, but I suppose you also knew that if you had the nerve then you could probably get away with anything. In a way I blame that bus conductor for me taking opium, becoming gay and not being able to visit Switzerland for the next twenty years.'

Nige said, 'I suppose it's a necessary evolutionary stage isn't it? Finding out that adults aren't omnipotent, the first phase of detaching from Mum or Dad and becoming an independent person.'

'Yeah – and I guess most people end up still more or less on speaking terms with their parents. But when you have the kind of claustrophobic relationship Stanley and his mum have, I wonder how that can end? Sometimes I think Stanley might be like the citizen of some repressive regime who's managed to get round the Internet censors and suddenly discovers the rest of the world sees their beloved leader not as a super hero but as a big fat joke in a stupid uniform. What happens to those countries?'

'When they realise the emperor is a fraud? Oh civil war, genocide, the collapse of society, that sort of thing.'

Stanley spent all of 28 December – the day after the vanquishing of Monty Crisp – with Mister Roberts. He got up early, before his mother, and took Mister Roberts down the valley to the next village. While they were away from her, he thought, at least his mum couldn't get him to beat anybody else up. Once there they had walked around for a bit giving people the creeps, then when Stanley tired of this they turned and headed up into the hills.

Out of sight of human habitation they climbed north and west across the mountains towards Mulhacén, the highest mountain in mainland Spain. They were making for the ski resort of Sierra Nevada, he'd had a great day out there one Christmas holiday with Simon's family. The boys had spent the day snowboarding and they'd all had a sing-song in the car on the way home.

Mister Roberts made easy work of the difficult ascent, travelling over the smooth, shiny, slate-covered slopes at speed, his footfall shattering bits of rock into razor-sharp needles as he ran. Higher up on the mountainside they passed across the top of a bowl-like valley at the bottom of which there was a tarn of startlingly turquoise water still unfrozen. To Stanley it looked like a single blue eye staring back up at them.

Eventually they arrived at the resort. Begun in the sixties and built entirely out of alpine concrete it had the appearance of a council estate that had been provided with a ridiculous number of restaurants and bars. Mister Roberts wandered amongst the skiers in their brightly coloured outfits. A lot of them felt strangely uncomfortable at the sight of a man in a dark suit in their midst: they wondered if he wasn't an undertaker who had come to attend to one of their number who'd skied into a tree. The creepy couple in the Victorian outfits who'd been prowling around town in the days just after Christmas had been hard enough to take, but this guy was somehow even more unsettling.

Inside the suit Stanley was finding it wasn't as much fun as he thought it would be. It was amazing to possess this incredible machine, to travel great distances and smash down trees but it made him feel lonely and detached just watching the effects of his actions on the screens inside Mister Roberts' head.

In a square in front of the chairlift there were clusters of metal tables served by various cafés and restaurants. At one of these Stanley saw his ex-best friend Simon together with his family, eating the long doughnuts called churros, dunking them in hot chocolate and laughing under a big red umbrella. Tipped up on his forehead Simon wore an enormous pair of yellow-tinted designer sunglasses as if he were a playboy member of the royal family of Monaco.

Stanley felt a desperate urge to go over and talk to Simon, to be part of his happy gang. Slowly Mister Roberts approached the little group and stood next to them, he even reached out his hand towards the other boy but of course he couldn't speak. Gradually becoming aware of the ominous, threatening presence standing mute beside them Simon's family fell into an uneasy silence.

'Daddy's feeling frightened,' whispered Simon's dad.

After a few more seconds Mister Roberts turned and walked back out into the snow.

Though it was only half past four, cold night had suddenly fallen. Still Nige and Laurence remained on the terrace of Noche Azul. Laurence felt a certain gratitude towards Nige for sitting with him during most of the day while he poured out his discontent, not that she had anything better to do. And it wasn't a particular trial for her. Nige was one of those people who found everybody on the planet equally fascinating. She could sit and talk for hours with the most unlikely, dull or terrible individuals – the local peasants, Ukrainian criminals, Liberal members of the European Parliament. 'We call this a spoon in my country,' he had once heard her say to a Moroccan farmer.

When he'd lived in London he'd had a circle of close friends, some gay guys certainly but a couple of married couples too. Their relationships had been forged and tempered through enduring all manner of crises together from watching lovers expire in hospital wards to the dawning of the realisation that Kylie was overrated. But by moving he'd lost them and in the village you couldn't be choosy. The only qualification for being somebody's friend in the village was that they were there and they hadn't seriously tried to rob you in the last year or two. Often that didn't seem like enough.

Laurence asked Nige, now just a blurred shape across the table, 'Do you ever wonder why we came here?'

'What, to Spain?'

'Yeah.'

'Er, how about a new life free from all the crappy stuff that tied you down back home: the weather, the government, friends who know you too well?'

'I guess, it's just that I sometimes wonder if we're not all a bit the same, us Brits. We congratulate ourselves that we're not like those oafs on the costas who don't speak Spanish, if anything we know the language and we know the culture better than the natives. Even so, we're never going to be a true part of the country we live in. I sometimes wonder if it's that that appeals to us. We're all people who can't quite engage with life, we're people who sit on the terrace and watch and, of course, drink. I wish once in a while that I could give myself entirely to somebody or something. Instead I hang on to my air of amused detachment like a life raft.'

'That's the closest thing we have to a philosophy though isn't it, "live and let live"?'

'Sometimes I wonder whether it isn't more "fuck up and let fuck up".'

'I'll tell you what,' Donna said to her son three days after the eviction, 'you know tomorrow's New Year's Eve, right? I fancy a trip into Granada, get out of this stinking valley and spend some of the money that old bastard Monty Crisp gave us.'

'Me and you?'

'Well, yeah, of course me and you . . . and Mister Roberts.'

'Oh . . . OK, sure.'

The next morning as Donna was about to climb behind the wheel of their ancient brown Nissan Patrol Stanley said, 'No, Mum, let me.'

'But you don't know how to drive,' she replied.

'I don't, but I've been exploring his features when I've been walking around and I'm pretty sure Mister Roberts does.'

As they drove through the outlying houses beyond the village walls, on a patch of land cleared for development they saw a circle of jeering English kids. In the centre was Simon, tears flooding down his face, and next to him was Runciman, who was cutting up the yellow-tinted designer sunglasses with a pair of pruning shears.

Most Spaniards wish for a good death, they do not want to expire as they imagine Scandinavians do, hooked up to tubes and pipes in some white-tiled sterilised room. Rather they would prefer to flame out in a showy and extravagant fashion, if possible taking their family with them.

All those who witnessed the Nissan Patrol that day as it hurtled at barely believable speeds down the valley's narrow roads and onto the motorway marvelled at the audacity of its driver. Some who caught a glimpse of him said later that they wondered whether in his old-fashioned suit and slicked-back hair the man wasn't perhaps the spirit of the great toreador, Manolito. Certainly, whoever he was, he must have had the most incredible reflexes to pilot the bulky, top-heavy brown car in the way he did. Now he was on the gravel verge, now he was rounding a sharp bend with two wheels hanging over the void, now he was on the wrong side of the road zinking in and out of oncoming traffic. Many an office drone in their workaday Seat or Renault whispered a silent 'Ole!' as the 4x4 Nissan tore off their wing mirror while overtaking at 150 kilometres an hour on the hard shoulder.

At first Donna screamed and hung on to the door handle, but after a while she relaxed and sat smiling vaguely at the world as it hurtled at supersonic speeds towards her.

In Britain roadworks are presaged by miles and miles of cones so that traffic is affected in all directions but in Spain sometimes the only warning that men were working on the carriageway was a mechanical dummy of a man stuck by the side of the road, dressed in a fluorescent lime suit and brandishing a red flag. They passed one such just before the Alhambra junction and Mister Roberts gave him a secret little wave, robot to robot.

Mister Roberts parked the car alongside the Rio Genil in a stand of cypress trees at the foot of the Alhambra Hill. Smoke gently curled from the overheated brakes as Donna took the arm of Mister Roberts and the two of them walked away from the Nissan upwards towards the shopping streets in the centre of town.

Donna and her companion spent the morning in the smart little clothes shops around the Plaza Bib Rambla. From time to time she would solicit his opinion about some prospective purchase. 'What do you think about this scarf?' she'd ask, then, when he just stood impassively looking at her she'd invent a reply, 'No, you're right. Orange isn't my colour.'

When she tried something on that she didn't like Donna would simply throw it on the floor, the shopowners would move to complain but the hulking presence of Mister Roberts always took away their courage at the last minute. They also found themselves surprisingly open to offers of a discount when the time came to pay.

As the cathedral clock struck twelve Donna sat down at an outside table of a café in the square by the cathedral and told Mister Roberts to go back to the car to drop off all the bags of shopping they'd accumulated while she had a coffee and a sandwich and smoked a cigarette. Watching his broad muscular back as he punched through the crowds of tourists Donna comforted herself with the thought that her going out with a robot who was really her son wasn't by a long way the weirdest relationship she'd ever been in.

After he'd dropped off the shopping at the car Mister Roberts walked swiftly up to the Generalife gardens that surrounded the Alhambra. In front of a clipped hedge he sat down on a marble bench and after a second Stanley climbed out of the back, the opening in the robot's torso masked by the hedge. Then he walked to a kiosk outside the palace of Charles V and bought a ham and cheese sandwich. Returning to the bench he sat down next to Mister Roberts to eat it.

His mum had forgotten that there was no way that he could eat while he was inside the robot, just as she seemed to forget that he was inside Mister Roberts at all, and told him all kinds of things that he didn't really want to know, stuff about her pretending to be a gynaecologist in front of one of her boyfriends for example.

Stanley found himself being troubled by a whole range of disquieting emotions and thoughts. Firstly the loneliness he'd experienced the day before up in the Sierra Nevada was still with him, plus he couldn't understand why he hadn't been allowed to simply enjoy this marvellous object he'd found. On the one hand he was pleased that Mister Roberts was making his mum so happy but it had given him a queasy feeling to do the things she'd ordered him to do to Monty Crisp.

Stanley thought to himself, 'I'm a kid. I'm not supposed to be able to do stuff like that to a grown-up.'

The whole situation made him miserable: he'd

been so excited when he'd found Mister Roberts but it was extraordinary how quickly his mum had taken him over so that now the whole state of affairs seemed like some sort of incredibly complicated problem.

There was a quality of unrestrained rage that Mister Roberts had brought about in his mum that he'd never seen before, and he was afraid of how much further she would go, or rather, how much further she would make *him* go.

When Mister Roberts returned to the Plaza Bib Rambla Donna said crossly, 'Where've you been?' Then, realising he couldn't reply, said, 'Never mind. I feel like having a look round the tourist tat now.'

They moved through the narrow streets of the Alcaicería, the sun-starved alleyways that had once been the Arab silk market at the very centre of Moorish Granada. To the tourists this place reeked of authentic Islamic Al Andalus, but had in fact been remodelled in the nineteenth century as arcades of purpose-built souvenir shops.

This was the area where the gypsy women gathered to try and sell the tourists sprigs of heather and worthless advice. Their leader was a stout woman of perhaps fifty called Maria Conchita y Christabal Oviedo de Antequera. In the streets and on her blog she gave the impression of a fierce pride in her Romany heritage, but secretly Maria Conchita often wondered why she bothered, all of her family with all their complicated scams and importunings and thieving made about as much money as if just one of them had got some sort of proper job, cleaning buses at the depot perhaps or selling sandwiches outside the bullring – but that wasn't the gypsy way. History hung heavy on her: until twenty years ago her family had lived in a cave about half a kilometre away in the Sacremonte – the Gypsy Quarter of Granada, but then after the floods the council had moved most of the *gitanos* out to apartments on the Poligano, the bleak wind-blown housing estate hard by the Southern ring road. Maria Conchita caught the bus into the centre of Granada every morning, six days a week to walk the streets forcing herself on the tourists who ambled through the narrow mediaeval streets. Pretending to tell their fortunes she would inform rangy Scandinavian girls in rapid heavily accented Spanish that they were going to marry a man called Paco and would give birth to seven children – four boys named Carlos, Pedro, Miguel and Ramon, and three girls named Juanita, Marta and Conchita Immaculada.

When she was surveying the herds of sightseers Maria Conchita often imagined herself to be a lion on the plains of Africa sniffing the wind for the scent of wildebeest. A tingling of the scalp drew her gaze to one particular couple, a pretty if hard-faced blonde woman hanging on the arm of a bigger older, dark-haired man in a suit. Many would have mistaken the woman for Dutch or Scandinavian but Maria Conchita knew right away that she was English. It was one of her skills that she was proudest of, her ability to deduce instantly the country of origin of any tourist. The man on the other hand, no for once she didn't know. Disappointed she thought to herself that she must be getting old. Maybe soon she wouldn't bother coming into town so often.

Suppressing her irritation the gypsy woman approached the pair with a confident walk and grabbing the hand of the blonde launched into her patter. 'Beautiful señorita let me unravel for you the mysteries of the planets that determine the future of—'

The gypsy woman was shocked when the foreigner took her hand back with a dismissive gesture and a cataract of abuse in perfect Andalusian Spanish with a couple of authentic *gitano* swear words thrown in for good measure. Now Maria Conchita, her previous self-doubt thrown aside, was determined to make a sale, so wriggling sideways she tried the man instead. Taking firm hold of his hand and gazing up into his face she began her patter, but as soon as she looked into his dead eyes and felt the cold lifeless touch of his fingers she instantly knew him for what he was. Over numberless centuries at night around the campfire the gypsies had told stories and many of the stories had concerned such as him. In the caves of the Sacremonte the tale, a particular favourite of Maria Conchita's, was told as if it had happened yesterday. It was a story of the old ghetto in Prague and the rabbi who brought to life a man made of mud.

'Golem!' Maria Conchita screamed in Romany, 'the golem is in the ghetto. Help! Help! The golem, the dybbuck has come here to Granada!'

Further up Calle Reyes Catolicos two of her cousins in the middle of picking the pockets of an Australian backpacker heard her cry and took it up; in a cave in the Sacremonte four of her uncles who'd been giving an appallingly inept flamenco show to some frightened Danes heard their relative and also took up the call. 'The golem is in the ghetto! The dybbuck has come here to Granada!' they cried and throwing down their guitars raced from the cave and headed down the hill and into town. On a patch of land below the Alhambra, where they ran a parking scam almost as old as the Alhambra itself, members of Maria Conchita's tribe heard the call and stripping off the luminous jackets they wore to lend them spurious veracity as parking attendants they too ran for the Alcaicería. Soon seemingly every gypsy in

Granada and the family of frightened Danes were running through the narrow streets, bowling over tourists as they ran. Before long there was a large mob of dark-skinned men and dirndl-skirted women brandishing knives and sticks, pouring down the alleyways of the old town and heading for the continuing screams echoing around the silk market. In the middle of the rabble Maria Conchita thought to herself, Yes this is what it is to be a gypsy. When you are threatened by a monster a single call and they come from all corners of the city to protect you.

As soon as the Gypsy woman began screaming Donna and Mister Roberts fled. At first they ran side by side, along the cobblestones of the ancient town, while in the distance the guttural cries of the gypsy mob grew louder by the second. Stanley realised that even with the power of Mister Roberts he would not be able to fight so many armed and determined people, so suddenly he pulled Donna to a stop.

'What are you doing?' she gasped, her eyes wide with fright.

Silently Mister Roberts grabbed Donna and threw her over his shoulder then began to run, faster than before, down the hill towards the safe territory of the Calle Colon and the newer nineteenth-century part of town with its big stores and fancy hotels, and where the gypsies would not venture.

As he fled, Donna, jolting up and down on Mister Roberts' shoulder, shouted insults at the pursuing mob.

'C'mon, you pack of bastards,' she yelled. 'My boyfriend would kill the lot of you if I told him to.'

Año Nuevo

It took the two of them several hours to circle back to their Nissan parked on the banks of the Rio Genil without being spotted by any gypsies and night was falling by the time they reached the battered brown car. Donna drove back to the valley sunk in thought while Stanley dozed inside the suit. Once they were back in the house and Mister Roberts was parked upstairs in Stanley's bedroom they convened a family meeting around the kitchen table. For once it was Stanley who spoke first. 'Well, we can't take him anywhere where there's gypsies.'

'Which means, more or less, any town in Spain,' Donna replied, glumly.

Stanley added, 'I don't think they'll bother us if we don't go too close. If they're like those other gypsies that used to come round to our house, Paco or Pedro or that one with the American car, then they're very superstitious, they'll only attack if they feel threatened, like geese . . .'

'So he's stuck here and we're stuck here with him. How am I going to make money out of him if he's stuck in the valley?'

Stanley felt a great relief flood through him and at the same time another realisation. Until that moment he hadn't known how desperately he had wanted his mother to accept there were restrictions on what Mister Roberts should do. If Mister Roberts was stuck in the valley it seemed a much better and safer outcome. Before his appearance there'd been a limit to how far his mother could go, after all she had to make a living and get served in the shops and stuff, so even if she wanted to, she couldn't fight with absolutely everybody, but he'd feared that with Mister Roberts by her side she'd get completely out of control. In the days since he'd found Mister Roberts he'd spent a lot of time wondering if he shouldn't be doing something special with his discovery. If his life was a comic book then Mister Roberts would be out there fighting crime or feeding the poor, not going around screwing people over, which seemed to be his mother's preferred option. At least he hoped after the problems in Granada his mum might drop any plans she'd had to profit from Mister Roberts by messing with people.

In a while Stanley left his mother drinking vodka in the kitchen and went upstairs to sleep. He felt really tired because Donna kept Mister Roberts up late into the night sitting beside her at Bar Noche Azul.

Earlier on when he'd taken the robot up to his bedroom he had sat him down on a wooden box facing the bed, now his last sight as he tumbled into sleep was the reassuring picture of Mister Roberts sitting watching over him as the church bells tolled in the New Year and rockets exploded across the night sky.

Next day in Bar Noche Azul the foreign community was nursing its collective New Year's hangover. Kirsten, the Dutch academic, returning to her seat from the toilets where she had been sick, said in her perfect English, 'Retrospectively it has to my mind been a curious Christmas holidays. Typified, if you will, by the arrival of that huge silent man Mister Roberts. Though I didn't see it, from what I'm told it was remarkable what he did to those two Russians and then his dragging Donna out and she being completely terrified then returning with her a few hours later all smiles, that is most peculiar. What's more the whole shebang occurring on Christmas Day.'

'Maybe he was Santa, spreading Christmas cheer,' Baz remarked, his words muffled because he was holding his head in his hands.

'More like Satan, from what I saw,' said Frank.

'Or Stan,' added Janet.

'Eh, Stan! What do you mean Stan?' Laurence asked looking up, his head fizzing with annoyance and unabsorbed alcohol.

'He looked a bit like my Uncle Stan,' Janet replied, smiling serenely.

Laurence felt a sudden stab of despair that he spent his life with these people, that was exactly the sort of thing that had him on his hands and knees crawling around the floor.

He was seriously contemplating hitting Janet when there was a scraping, scuffling sound at the door and a large black man entered the bar, bent under the weight of a huge canvas bag hanging from his shoulder.

In the big cities or the coastal resorts there were many Africans just like him who walked from bar to bar offering for sale pirated CDs, cheap sunglasses, crappy jewellery or knock-off DVDs, but up here in the mountains they were rarer, and as the pickings were thinner only the most desperate worked this remote valley. Two weeks before, Samuel, the big boss, had driven Adey and three other men in his BMW from Algeciras to a village much lower down the valley and told them he would pick them up in twenty days' time. Until then they would walk from village to village, sleeping in the fields or in *cortijos* at night and during the day attempting to sell the goods that Samuel provided for them at a substantial mark-up.

As soon as he stepped into the bar the British launched a chorus of aggrieved bleating at him. 'Adey, that *Best Bob Dylan* CD I bought off you had the same track on it twelve times and it sounded like it was sung by a Chinese man in a shed,' said Baz.

'Adey, that Windows XP you sold me set my computer on fire,' moaned Miriam.

'Adey, those sunglasses were backwards,' complained Frank.

Only Laurence and Nige remained silent since they never bought any items from Adey. Laurence never purchased his shabby products because as someone who worked in the entertainment community (however infrequently these days), he would have nothing to do with piracy and Nige never bought from him because she wasn't an idiot.

'Yes, yes,' Adey replied smiling sweetly, 'yes, yes, as I've told you before all complaints must be addressed to the head office in Lagos.' Adey often wondered what they thought they were getting for five Euros. Then rather than spreading out his wares as anticipated he said, 'Mister Laurence, I would like to have a little word with you on the terrace.'

'Merry Christmas, Mister Laurence,' whispered Nige as after a few seconds' pause Laurence unsteadily got out of his chair and crossed to the front door and the wintry sunlight beyond it.

'If I'm not back in an hour don't send a search party,' he told the group with a sickly smile.

As he emerged blearily into the daylight Adey was already seated at one of the tables under the vine-covered terrace, bare of leaves at this time of year. The watery light filtering through the stout tendrils stippled the rusty furniture like camouflage.

'Can I get you a drink?' Laurence asked nervously, sitting down next to the African. 'A cocktail, perhaps?'

'No, no thank you, I do not drink.'

'Really? I didn't know that.'

Taking a breath Adey began, 'Mister Laurence I have always respected you. I respected you because you do not buy rubbish from me. You and the lady who likes other ladies. So, because I respect you now I have something extremely important to ask you.'

'Yes?'

Adey reached into his pocket and brought out a square of plastic and passed it to Laurence. 'Tell me, Mister Laurence, have you seen this man?'

Laurence found himself staring at a photograph

of Donna's new friend Mister Roberts standing stiffly inside some sort of glass tube. 'No,' he said after a second's pause, 'I've never seen him.' And handed the piece of plastic back to the African. It occurred to him, even as he lied, that a truly first-rate hangover such as his, which dulled the senses, was a great thing to have when you didn't want to tell somebody clever the truth. Laurence said to himself that in denying knowledge of Mister Roberts he was simply and automatically following an important tradition of life in the village. When inquisitive people – the Guardia Civil, private detectives, wives, husbands, defrauded timeshare investors – came round searching for somebody, an event that happened with remarkable frequency, everybody, both British and Spanish always automatically denied their existence. Like the foreign legion, they said, '*El no existe.*'

He got the feeling that Adey wasn't entirely convinced by his protestation of ignorance but was also certain that there was no way for the African to penetrate the bleary disconnection he was feeling.

Looking into his eyes Adey said, 'It is really important that this man is found, Mister Laurence. I can't emphasise that enough.'

Putting the photo back in his pocket he continued, 'This man, he is very, very dangerous, more dangerous than you can possibly imagine. If you do see him I would like you to fire three rockets to the east in rapid succession or I suppose you could send an SMS text message to my mobile phone, but reception in the high country can be very poor. At the moment that is my base of operations – up in the high country in the caves where they say the last Moors hid from the inquisition.'

'Yes, of course, Adey. I'll definitely be in touch if I see him,' Laurence replied, not really paying attention to what was being said. He was beginning to panic now, fearing that his hangover must be reaching new depths of toxicity because it had just come back to him that a few seconds before when he'd looked at the picture of Mister Roberts, even though it was on a flat piece of plastic the image had appeared to be moving; the camera or whatever it was that had recorded the image had been circling the glass tube round and around giving a clear 3-D view of the front and back of the big man's head. Laurence had never experienced that particular side effect of alcohol poisoning before: three dimensionality. If he was starting to have such delusions could the bats in the walls be far behind?

Adey was sorting through his bag of junk prior to leaving when Miriam came out onto the terrace. 'So, Adey,' she said flirtatiously, swaying a little from side to side, 'have you got anything special for little old Miriam?'

'Oh, I do have something but I'm not sure you'll want it,' Adey replied. As he spoke, for some reason the African looked directly at Laurence.

'Ooh what is it? What is it?' Miriam said.

The black man reached into his bag and came out holding a strange-looking pair of headphones.

'With these headphones you can hear the thoughts of cats and dogs,' Adey stated simply.

'Really?' Miriam said, her eyes wide. 'That's always been my dream.'

'Well, now you can do it. Sadly they don't work on human-to-human transmission. You can't read people's thoughts, only animals'.'

'Who would want to know what people were thinking?' the woman asked, perplexed. Then, 'How much?'

'Five Euros, as always.'

Miriam quickly produced a five-euro note from her pocket and handed it over. In return she got the headphones.

Adey said, 'You just look at the animal you wish to communicate with, Miriam, then you will hear its thoughts.' As he rose he addressed Laurence, 'Remember, Mister Laurence, that man is more dangerous than you can possibly know.' Then he left, slinging his heavy bag over his shoulder and walking down Calle Santo Segundo towards the main gate in the ancient wall and the path that led to the high country.

After watching him trudge out of sight Laurence and Miriam re-entered the gloom of Noche Azul. Miriam excitedly told everyone, 'These headphones. Apparently with these headphones I can hear the thoughts of cats and dogs. I'm going to try them on now.' She placed the device over her springy grey hair. The phones didn't quite fit her ears as if they were made for a different, smaller shape of head but with a bit of bending she forced them until they were close enough.

'Now I look at a dog . . .' said Miriam turning her head around until she finally fixed on her own three-legged pet Coffee Table lying on the cold tiled floor of the bar. As soon as Miriam's gaze alighted on the creature Laurence and the others heard a sound like a bad-tempered radio play leaking out of the earphones and a terrible expression of fear came over Miriam's face. Frantically she tried to tear the headphones from her head but at first she couldn't dislodge them, until finally, she managed to rip them off, fling them to the floor and stamp the device into a thousand pieces with her tiny feet. Then she screamed at all the dogs in the bar, 'You bastards! You little bastards!' Then she ran out of the door. Naturally her dog went after her, travelling remarkably rapidly on its three legs and, because Coffee Table was leaving, several other dogs followed. For quite some time as she ran through the narrow lanes of the village they could all hear Miriam screaming, 'No you bastards get away from me! How could you? How could you think those things? I feed you! I feed all of you swine!' and as she ran the pack of barking hounds pursuing her grew ever larger.

It took Adey two hours of walking along dusty rock-strewn paths before he finally reached the mouth of a cave hidden from view in a stand of cork oaks and cactus. He entered the cave and gave out a low whistle. Immediately there was a rustle from behind him, a pile of sacking stirred and from beneath it came two aliens both about the same size as a thirteen-year-old child.

Sitting quietly in the opposite corner, not quite covered by a blue tarpaulin, were a Victorian gentleman in a tall top hat and stiff tight suit with black patent leather boots on his feet and next to him his lady, golden curls spilling out from under a pink bonnet, gigantic hooped skirt flaring out from her waist and a frilly parasol held daintily over her shoulder.

*   *   *

Towards morning on Christmas Day Sid and Nancy's little shuttle craft had been impelled through the earth's atmosphere by the fireball of their mothership exploding under the remorseless assault of the rebel fighters. In a daze they landed their ship as near as they could to the spot where the deserter's craft was recorded as having touched down.

Since the moment when they'd been born in the military hatchery Sid and Nancy had lived a life of rigorous discipline and were unaccustomed to having to make any decisions for themselves; unsure of what to do next they sat for a while in stunned silence while the engines of their craft cooled and clicked behind them.

'The Imperial battlestar is destroyed,' said Sid finally. 'So what are we to do?'

'Carry on with the mission, of course,' Nancy replied.

She had come six hundred and ninety thousand places above Sid at the military academy so considered herself superior to him, even though they were equal in rank.

'But the Empire will have no record of the disappearance of the Planetary Exploration Suit and they will not know that we are trapped on this primitive planet,' Sid persisted, 'and we have no way to get in touch with headquarters. Perhaps if another battlecruiser is passing close by we could contact it with our communications equipment, but it could be years before that happens.'

'So we have no option but to complete our assigned task,' Nancy insisted.

Sid really couldn't see the logic of this, but unable to come up with a reply he went along with Nancy in finding a cave and hiding their ship at the back of it.

Then, following their last orders, the pair of aliens quickly set about trying to track down the missing Exploration Suit.

Despite Nancy's fixidity of purpose this did not go well. They soon found out as they travelled around the mountain villages of the Sierra Nevadas and Sierra de Contraviesas that a Victorian gentleman in a tall top hat accompanied by a lady with golden curls spilling out from under a pink bonnet and carrying a parasol, wordlessly showing their 3-D photo of Mister Roberts, did not meet with a great deal of cooperation.

As there was no resupply from the mothership their stocks of food soon began to run low. They were only a couple of days into their mission and already starving to death. Now it was Nancy's turn to be indecisive: there were no precedents for their predicament in the military training manuals and it was Sid who, by accident, came up with what they should do.

In some ways the aliens were obviously more advanced than human beings, their technology was clearly far in advance of anything that had been created on Earth. On the other hand, having only ever known constant warfare, fighting and struggle they were in some ways closer to their primitive natures. Sitting on the edge of the cave one morning Sid saw a jack rabbit skipping across the rocky grassland. More or less without a thought he pounced on the startled animal and killed it with his claws.

With astonishing rapidity ancient instincts began to emerge. Within five days of landing they had permanently shed their bulky human suits, and putting their mission to one side they began to hunt for sustenance. Lightning fast the pair ran across the hills catching rabbits and small birds to eat. For the first time in their lives they felt a sense of freedom, the destruction of the gigantic death star, symbol of Imperial power, of thoughtless devotion to duty, had shown them their natural selves, which they never could have conceived of when they were breathing the dead air of the giant spaceship. After all, as they said to each other, they had to be fit and healthy if at some future date they were going to find the deserter and the missing Planetary Exploration Suit.

It was during one of their hunting trips that they

came face to face with Adey. He was tramping between one village and another his bag of cheap junk on his back when he saw two large lizard-skinned creatures, one with a dead rabbit in its mouth. This was the first native that Sid and Nancy had encountered without the protection of their suits but they felt no reason to worry over meeting a lone human in this isolated place, after all they came from a culture that ruled most of the galaxy so they were merely curious to see what an inhabitant of this planet had to offer them.

On Adey's part he was unafraid partly because it was simply not in his nature to be intimidated by anyone but also because of a quirk in his character that had meant he had always been considered peculiar back home, because even as a child he had loved animals.

Everybody of importance, the preachers and the politicians, told the modern African that all creatures, all plants, all of nature was merely a resource for all-important, all-conquering mankind; any other feeling for the planet was dismissed as old-fashioned and outmoded sentimentality. Any animals that got in the way of intensive agriculture or chemical plants or prestigious dam-building schemes were to be exterminated, apart from those that were nice to eat or were of the bigger, furry kind that could be kept in parks for white tourists to visit.

This had always felt wrong to Adey and back when he was a child in his home village he had found a monitor lizard which had had one of its legs hacked off by local kids. Adey had nursed the creature back to health and kept it as a pet for many years so when he was confronted by two scaly creatures the size of a thirteen-year-old child, he was merely reminded of his former pet and felt only a benign curiosity.

Using sign language Sid and Nancy persuaded Adey to follow them to the cave where they had been sheltering and once there, employing headphones identical to the ones he'd sold Miriam that allowed different species to talk to each other, the aliens and the African were able to communicate with each other.

Over the next day and a half as they sat round the fire feasting on rabbit and wild capers Adey told them all about his life: the poverty in his home country, his trip across the rough seas from the Spanish colony of Melilla to Alicante in a leaking fishing boat and the work he did trudging from village to village, trying to sell pirated junk. In turn they told him all about their home planet, the Empire and the galactic wars, the many technological marvels they possessed and every detail of their mission including the bit about the Earth being destroyed if they didn't succeed in locating the missing Alien Exploration Suit and if they managed to contact another Imperial Battlestar. The preachers back home had often gone on about the Earth being destroyed so it didn't come as a particular shock to Adey that it might actually happen, but he still felt on balance that it would be a good idea if Mister Roberts was found, so he suggested to Sid and Nancy that he should undertake the task of finding the robot. With nothing to lose the two aliens agreed and handed over the 3-D picture of their quarry.

Tres Reyes

The Christmas and New Year holidays ground on like some kind of demented gameshow from Italian television where the objective was not to go to bed ever and to absorb as much drink and drugs as possible. In former times the festivities would have been a brief respite from the endless backbreaking toil of life on the land but these days, when most people's work seemed easy and undemanding, with all kinds of power tools and electronic devices to help them, the Spanish appeared determined to drink and eat more and stay up later than they ever had before.

Even so there was a limit. Once the holidays were over a lot of the community, both British and Spanish, would gratefully disappear behind their studded gates, metal window grills and high walls until the spring, but before they could do that they had to get through the festival of Three Kings on the evening of 5 January, the holiday on the 6th then finish with the Matanza the day after.

So there was still just under a week to go when on the evening of the 2nd the whole gang of Brits drove ten kilometres down the valley to another settlement where they were having a fiesta. To squeeze in a fiesta between Christmas, New Year's and Three Kings might seem odd but there simply weren't enough days in the year for the number of fiestas the modern Spaniard wanted to throw. Sometimes when Laurence drove to Granada or Malaga on the motorway it seemed as if half the commercial traffic was merry-go-rounds and doughnut stalls being towed from town to town by groaning, smoke-belching old trucks. The other half was eighteen-wheel tractor-trailers hauling prawns up and down the country.

This place they were driving to was a town rather than a village and the last community before the Granada/Motril highway, which ran across the end of the main street on an arched concrete bridge. After a few weeks stuck in the house Laurence often felt driving down the main street of the town with its huge grey shed of an orange cooperative, Internet café and two discos that he'd suddenly emerged onto

Fifth Avenue or Piccadilly, so frantic and twenty-first century did it seem.

Of late, though, during the last three or four years, he had found himself, more and more, avoiding the place. When Laurence had first come to live in Spain, when the only foreign inhabitants had been Roger, Nige and Baz and himself, he'd frequently driven to the town in his little Seat. Before high-speed broad-band there had been the bank to visit to change money or make deposits and the post office to send letters and now and then he had just wanted to hear the voice of another English person. In time it slowly dawned on Laurence that each time a new individual came to live in his own village, an almost identical Brit seemingly appeared by magic in this town. In their 'Bar Harlequin', almost identical to Noche Azul, with the same harsh neon lighting, screaming stereo and giant TVs in each corner, this British community possessed their own Miriam, their own Leonard, their own Baz the builder, their own Janet, their own Frank and even, he had to admit, their own Laurence – a prissy set designer by the name of Derek Twookey with whom he'd worked years before on a series of *Lovejoy*. Of course there were differences: the town's Li Tang was a Cambodian woman called Dao and their Nige, an ex-model called Magenta de Calliope, wasn't a lesbian.

After some internal wrestling Laurence had forced

himself to come to terms with this duplication and the realisation that came with it that he wasn't a unique snowflake, that there were maybe hundreds of Laurences in southern Spain alone. It took some getting used to, but he eventually managed it. However, since the turn of the century something more disturbing had begun: there had started to appear not just versions of him and his friends but younger versions of him and his friends. Right now in this town there was a whole crowd of young British who were to his eyes clearly Laurence and Nige and Baz and Miriam when they had been in their twenties. That was much harder to take. To see yourself happy and healthy, laughing and optimistic, with all your myriad blunders and adventures ahead of you, stripped away the defences you had laboriously built up against the depredations of old age, like brake fluid thrown over the paint of a car by a jealous lover. Apart from the pain of seeing yourself as you once were, there was also the feeling that these young people were your responsibility in some way, that somehow you could prevent them making the mistakes you made so that their lives wouldn't descend into the same sadness as yours. Once at an earlier fiesta, very drunkenly he had gone up to the guy he thought was Laurence Version 2.0 and said, 'Don't wear brown shoes to the BAFTAS,' but of course the boy hadn't known what he was talking about and had simply sidled away from him with a look of disgust on his face.

Their dopplegangers were at the fiesta tonight, grouped around a circular white plastic table, but luckily they were the ones who were the same age. Laurence supposed the younger ones were off somewhere else, perhaps actually having a good time.

So identical to his own gang did this little group appear that he found himself looking to see where their mute, frightening giant was, but of course this town possessed no Mister Roberts. One up to his village, then.

In most ways the fiesta in this town, like its British community, was identical to the fiestas in all the other villages, towns and cities in all of the other valleys of the Sierra Nevada. The same band played in the same tent and the same stallholders sold fried dough and plastic trinkets. Yet there were also always some subtle differences. In this particular town they had a legend that sometime in the distant past there had lived a duck which had saved the town from marauding Visigoths with its loud, warning quacks. Due to this fable the church always had several Barbary ducks wandering up and down the aisles and honking their way through the priest's sermon. Also at fiesta time the village men would dress up in elaborate duck outfits that would be burnt at the end of the night on a big bonfire. Despite this it had been discovered at some point that being dressed like a duck did not provide the villagers with enough opportunity to make a huge noise, so now in one hand each fowl carried an antique flintlock pistol. From time to time they would fire this gun in the air with a terrifying percussion that sent dangerous shards of shrapnel and bits of the pistol flying in all directions.

Laurence's gang found themselves a table on the edge of the dance floor. He had never mentioned his doppleganger theory to anyone except Nige and she'd dismissed it as a symptom of his overactive imagination. Nige could see no similarities between the Brits in this town and their own crowd, but he noticed that they naturally chose a table as far away from their doubles as possible. Frank went to the bar to buy the cloakroom tickets that could be exchanged for drinks and then they settled down in the distinctive atmosphere of the Spanish fiesta – the air heavy with the smell of doughnuts and gunpowder.

Laurence leant across to Donna who was sitting opposite him. 'Do you fancy a dance?' he asked.

'You want to dance with me, Laurence?' Donna replied with surprise.

'Yes, if Mister Roberts doesn't mind.'

'Oh, he doesn't mind.' She turned to the hulk, 'Do you mind me dancing with Laurence, sweetie?'

The hulk made no reply so taking Laurence's hand

Donna led him towards the dance floor and the deafening Latin American beats of Humana Show 2000.

Laurence took her in his arms. It made him feel melancholic recalling the fiestas in the past where they'd danced together. With Donna, once she'd broken with you, her anger was such that there was no way back. She might act friendly if it suited her but she'd never shine that bright light on you ever again. He, on the other hand, was never able to let even the smallest thing go: there were feuds he'd had with people going back to primary school and there were ex-lovers from whom he was still demanding an explanation, sometimes in front of their wives and children, as to why they broke up with him. Laurence supposed that this reluctance to let go, this inability to acknowledge when a relationship was over, was why he felt he had to warn Donna over, the danger he thought her boyfriend might be bringing down on her.

As they slowly circled the wooden floor Laurence said, 'You know Adey?'

'The darkie who goes around selling stuff? Yeah, I bought a hairdryer off him once that turned out to have its insides made of waste paper.'

'The African, yes. Well, he came to me yesterday in Noche Azul and showed me a photo of your friend Mister Roberts and told me that he was really dangerous, that people were looking for him and if

I knew where Mister Roberts was I should alert Adey by firing three rockets into the air.'

'I see, yeah.' She paused thoughtfully, then said, 'OK. So what?'

'So do you know any reason why people should be looking for him? I mean how much do you know about him, have you asked him where he's come from, what he's doing here?'

Laurence had expected she would at least consider what he was telling her but with a confident, silly smile Donna merely said, 'You know we don't pry into other people's business in our village, Laurence. I don't ask you why you can't ever go back to Switzerland now, do I?'

Laurence sighed. 'I know but I thought we always had a limit about who we allowed to live in the village: VAT fraud, OK; sexual offences that are only illegal in the Southern states of the US, fine; dodgy passport, all right . . . but there is something about that man that is truly disturbing.'

Seemingly changing the subject she asked him, 'Laurence, you've met lots of rich, powerful people over the years haven't you?'

'Yeah, I suppose so.'

'Were they nice?'

'Nice?'

'Yeah: nice, polite, interested in what other people had to say. Nice.'

'Well, no, they weren't by and large. Very occasionally they would be OK, polite and thoughtful but then you'd really notice it and it would usually pass and they'd go back to being not nice.'

'Exactly,' Donna said. 'My dad once told me that poor people had to be nice to each other because they might want to borrow somebody's van one day. But the rich, they can buy their own van, can't they?'

'Well, I don't know what Julia Roberts would want with a van, but I suppose you're right.'

'And don't you think that in fact rich people are being more human really, more authentic, because that's what we'd all be like if we had proper power, if our lives weren't in the hands of others?'

'Are we still talking about the loan of commercial vehicles?' Laurence asked.

Ignoring him, Donna continued. 'You know, I used to worry like mad if people liked me or not. I was terrified of being alone, abandoned, friendless, because the world seemed like such a frightening place that you had to have allies but I'll tell you what, Grandad, now I've got Mister Roberts the world needs to be frightened of me.'

At the same time as Donna was dancing with Laurence and explaining her ideas of evolutionary psychology, her secret weapon was being forced to listen to Miriam drunkenly telling him all the details of her mental breakdown. There was something about the stillness of the big man that encouraged some people, those whose brains weren't put together right, to confide in him.

'Is it wrong for a woman to want to have a child by her cat?' Miriam woozily demanded.

With the use of hand gestures Mister Roberts indicated that he had to go somewhere immediately and without waiting for Miriam to tell him any more he got up and striding through the dancers was soon far away from the clamour of the dance floor.

On the southern edge of the town there was a stone bridge that spanned an *arroyo* and carried the old coaching road that ran from Granada to the coast. Mister Roberts headed towards this. The robot's footsteps echoed from the walls of the town's long shopping street, empty since all the inhabitants had been drawn to the noise and excitement of the fiesta. In the distance as he walked Mister Roberts saw Runciman Carnforth heading back into town after huffing a can of lighter gas under the bridge.

Under a streetlight they came together, Mister Roberts and the boy. Runciman went to pass but Mister Roberts stepped in front of the thirteen-year-old, blocking his way and putting a hand on his chest. Runciman was vaguely aware of who this man was, having seen him around the valley, so he wouldn't have been particularly worried even if he hadn't been high.

As it was, the bully simply stared placidly up into the dark eyes of the man, expecting that at some point he'd ask a question or tell him off about some misdemeanour but instead the big adult merely withdrew his hand and brushing him aside walked towards the darkness of the countryside.

'Goodnight, boss!' Runciman called after him.

Rapidly Stanley parked Mister Roberts underneath the bridge with his back to the rough dripping stone, then he climbed out, scrambled back up the dirt bank and re-entered the town.

As he walked Stanley thought to himself, shouldn't there be some warm glow of goodness burning in his chest? To have let Runciman go on his way was a really big thing for him and yet he felt, what? Nothing really, well maybe if he thought about it he didn't feel bad, not particularly good but not bad.

When he'd done a bad thing, like helping his mother mess with Monty or beating up Sergei, there had been a kind of mad pleasure to it but it had been tinged with blackness at the edges in a way that this feeling wasn't.

'Bloody Hell!' he thought. 'Is that it? Is that the best you could hope for if you were really good and didn't abuse your power over terrible bullies who in anybody's book deserved to be well smashed-up. The absence of bad?'

* * *

In the long and forgotten centuries before the British came to southern Spain the things that affected life in the valley were the simple, timeless elements of rural existence: the weather, disease, feuds and family disputes, the wholesale price of oranges. Excepting the upheaval of the civil war even changes of government in distant Madrid had had little effect. Yet in the twenty-first century these little white villages strung out along a twisting mountain road on the edge of the high sierras were in certain ways more connected to Crouch End than to Cordoba. In the last few years the holiday times of private schools in Britain had become as important a component of village life as the almond harvest. The numbers of kids running around the squares, lanes and paths would be swollen considerably throughout the duration of the winter, easter or summer breaks by the children of those who owned second homes within the walls of the village or out in the surrounding countryside.

Many of the parents of these youngsters were powerful people back in the UK, TV producers, surgeons, hedge-fund managers, successful publishers. They spent huge amounts of money sending their children to private schools in order to ensure that they mixed only with the offspring of people identical to themselves. Yet curiously, when they came to the village, these same powerful parents took no notice of what their sons and daughters were up to, so that unsupervised they came into contact with all kinds of youths from all kinds of possibly unsavoury backgrounds. A couple of summers back the two daughters of Fabien, the co-owner of Noche Azul, had spent a fortnight staying in London with a Channel 4 commissioning editor and his two teenage girls. The village girls found most things about London unimpressive including being part of the audience for the recording of a top comedy gameshow and dinner at the Ivy Restaurant where they sat next to Elton John's boyfriend, but all the girls would cherish for ever the afternoon the four of them got together with Baz's three children who lived with his estranged wife and her new boyfriend on a council estate in Hackney and the whole gang had spent seven hours travelling around the West End of London surreptitiously disposing of the separate parts of a sawn-off shotgun that had been used to rob a post office.

Stanley walked back through the press of drunken adults attending the fiesta, down to the schoolyard where he knew most of the younger people would be hanging out. In the crush of kids milling around the stalls was a girl called Pepper Fawkes. Pepper's father was a solicitor in the West Midlands who specialised in getting footballers off charges of rape, drug possession and dangerous driving. During the last few holidays Stanley had been one of a crowd of kids who'd been allowed to hang around their big house on the edge of the village, to enjoy its pool in the summer and its central heating and satellite TV in the winter. Though Pepper herself had never given him much attention he felt a fondness towards her because her parents had continued to be nice to him after they'd had the inevitable falling out with his mum.

Catching sight of her Stanley wondered whether Pepper had always possessed those small breasts and long glossy chestnut hair and whether she'd always been so tall. He seemed to remember in the summer she'd been chubby and worn childish dresses, but it might have been that back then he hadn't found every centimetre of her as unbelievably fascinating as he did right now. Seeing somebody over his shoulder Pepper detached herself from the crowd of English girls and came in his direction with a sinuous walk he couldn't take his eyes off, then to his surprise she came and stood right in front of him, her little feet planted apart sheathed in trainers he'd seen advertised on the TV. 'I bet you can't run as fast as me,' Pepper said.

Stanley was astonished that she was talking to him, as far as he could remember they'd never had a conversation of any kind, but he quickly replied, 'I bet I can.'

'All right, I'll race you to the Ermita then.'

The Ermita was a small chapel built on a rocky hill about a kilometre and a half outside the village and reached by a narrow dirt path that wound through the orange groves.

Without looking at him or saying another word Pepper set off at a run, her whippy body dodging through the clumps of families who were hanging round the stalls. Stanley charged after her and soon they were out of the settlement and deep into the silent countryside, the white of her T-shirt flickering ahead of him in the moonlight. Slowly he gained on her but she still arrived ahead of him at the chapel where she slumped breathless on a bench. Stanley joined her and they sat gulping in the cold night air until after a few minutes the girl's breathing calmed and she said,

'I won.'

'Yes, you did.'

Looking sideways at him she asked, 'So who's that bloke that's been hanging around with your mum?'

'You mean Mister Roberts?'

' Yeah, him. My dad says he's the most frightening-looking man he's ever seen and if we were back home he'd inform social services and they'd have you taken into care.'

'Just as well this is my home then,' Stanley said. 'He's wrong about Mister Roberts anyway, he just looks hard. But he's all right really, when you get to know him.'

'Honest? My mum said that black guy who sells stuff was looking for Mister Roberts. Apparently, according to what she heard in the bar, he showed Laurence a picture and said he was really dangerous and if he saw him he should fire three rockets in the air or find him in some cave he's living in, up where the Moors had their last stand.'

'Well, people really shouldn't interfere because he's not dangerous or anything. I know he looks rough and frightening on the outside but inside, believe me, he's a very kind person, good-hearted and honest.'

'Really? Nobody else seems to think that.'

'They don't know him like I do and if you'd met some of my mum's other boyfriends . . .'

'I guess so,' Pepper said, losing interest in Mister Roberts, then pushing herself off from the rock she asked, 'So you want to race back to the fiesta or do you want to stay here and hold hands for a bit?'

The night after the duck fiesta Stanley came downstairs to the kitchen and jumped at the sight of Mister Roberts sitting at the table with a Santa hat on his head, a long brightly coloured red silk scarf from Morocco around his neck and some pink and green knitted gloves on his hands. He'd forgotten that he and his mum had dressed the robot in his Christmas presents the night before. Donna had bought the scarf at Nige's shop and the gloves had been purchased by Stanley at the Al Campo supermarket on the coast. It was a measure of how happy Mister Roberts had made his mum that she'd suspended her ban on Christmas.

Last night he'd thought Mister Roberts looked jolly and festive, but now the big man appeared sort of sad to Stanley, like a guy who had no friends and was spending the Christmas holidays alone in a cold and shabby house.

Searching in the larder he saw that there was nothing that even vaguely resembled fresh bread so putting on his padded jacket and woolly hat he headed for the *panaderia*.

The old ladies who baked the bread in the ancient house on the corner of Calle Santo Segundo always made a big fuss of him and gave him a free cake as well as the loaf he bought.

Donna was lying face down on top of the bed still in the clothes she'd worn the night before. There was no heating in the house so she woke shivering from the cold as the sound of the door slamming behind Stanley shook her from sleep. Painfully she crawled under the duvet, undressed and pulled on a greasy T-shirt she found beneath her pillow, then she dragged the duvet over her head and imagined she was buried in a snowdrift.

Donna struggled to remember the night before at the fiesta, obviously the images of giant ducks lumbering about had actually happened, but there were other darker and more distorted figures that loomed on the edge of her memory that she couldn't figure out whether they were real or not.

Underneath her jagged headache and mouth swamped with bile Donna's thoughts were unhappy. Her dad had been fascinated by history. One of the things she could remember him saying often was that while the Chinese had discovered gunpowder they had only used it to make fireworks, stupid pinwheels and rockets. It had taken the genius of the Western mind to apply gunpowder to the rifle, the grenade and the machine-gun. To use it to enslave the entire world. She thought she was behaving like the Chinese right now, with Mister Roberts. And letting down her dad in a way, wherever he was. She needed that leap of inspiration, that rush of genius, to discover what to do with this astounding gift from outer space.

Time was particularly crucial because if what Laurence had said was true then there were people after him. In some way she needed to make herself and Mister Roberts invincible right away. Then her dad would see she was worth something.

When she had a hangover her son would go walking in the mountains for most of the day to keep out of her way, so she assumed she would be alone for some time to think about the future, therefore she was annoyed to hear him return so soon. After some crashing and banging in the kitchen he came into her room with a tray on which was coffee and half of the loaf toasted in two long slices.

'Hi Mum, I've made you some breakfast,' he said.

Throwing back the cover and wincing at the sudden movement Donna saw he'd taken the Santa hat off Mister Roberts and put it on his own head. Stanley laid the tray on the bedside table, then rather than withdrawing as she'd hoped, he sat at the end of her bed looking at her with his big, annoying brown eyes.

Donna raised herself and picking up the coffee cup, rapidly cooling in the cold mountain air of the bedroom, put it to her lips, hoping to stave off whatever it was that he wanted to tell her. 'Mmm,' Donna said. 'Nice coffee.'

It was no use, Stanley wouldn't be deflected. He said in a rush, 'Mum, I don't want to use Mister Roberts anymore.'

Donna kept her nose buried in the coffee cup for a few seconds composing her thoughts. 'What do you mean you don't want to use him?' she finally asked.

'I mean I don't want to be inside him, or to do stuff with him. Do you know what I mean? I don't think we should be using him the way we have been. I keep worrying, what if he was sent to us as a test? Like in all those Bible stories where everybody always does the wrong thing then God punishes them by turning them into frogs or whatever. I'm scared, Mum. He's too powerful.'

Donna, her thoughts churning, eventually said, 'Of course, babe, if it makes you unhappy then we'll just hide him somewhere and leave him alone.'

Stanley let out a trembling breath. 'Really, Mum? Do you mean it?'

'Of course I do, darling. After all, you being happy is the most important thing, isn't it?'

A big smile spread across his face. 'Aww, thanks Mum. You'll see – this'll be much better for everybody.' Then he leaned across and hugged her.

'Well, no mother wants to make her son miserable. Now why don't you go out for a walk or something?'

'Yeah, cheers Mum, you're the best.' So saying Stanley slid off the bed, ran down the stairs and out of the door.

Wearily Donna threw the duvet back and touched her feet to the freezing tiled floor. She was going to have to go out after all.

'That's the thing about soup: every mouthful's the same as the last,' said Lady Jennifer de Saint Cloud

Von Rumminger, Duchess of Bolton and Viscountess Carnforth, better known to Stanley as Runciman's mum.

She and Donna were having the set lunch at a roadside restaurant off the old road to Granada just beyond the pass of Suspiro del Moro, known in English as the Moor's Last Sigh. This was the spot from where Boabdil, the last Muslim king of Granada, surveying the lands he had lost to the Catholic Monarchs Ferdinand and Isabella wept, at which point his mother helpfully turned to him and said, 'Now you weep like a woman over what you could not defend as a man!'

There was a nice restaurant and a branch of the DIY chain Polanco there these days.

Jennifer Carnforth still lived with her four children in the farmhouse from where her husband had led the religious cult that had only recently been broken up by the special squad of the Guardia Civil.

Amongst the Brits her home was universally referred to as 'The Funny Farm', because it was the oddest house that anybody had ever seen, which was really saying something – in these parts the title had some serious contenders. There seemed to be some madness that seized people when they moved to Spain and set about building their dream home. Indeed, that is often what they come to resemble, houses that were only ever seen in dreams, of a disturbing kind.

Amongst the British community only Laurence and Nige lived in dwellings that followed conventional notions of interior design with walls and doors and windows where you'd expect them to be, everybody else's house possessed at least one aberration – a hen house in the living room or an open-air toilet on the roof but even they had to admit that Jennifer Carnforth's place went far beyond anything envisioned even in their wildest fantasies.

From the outside the Funny Farm was relatively conventional, a jumble of buildings that leaned against each other with crenellated battlements, walls of wood, concrete and stone and in parts roofing of thatch, tile and corrugated iron. It was inside where the real madness began. The interior walls were painted incompetently in scumbled blues, reds and yellows as if infected with psychedelic mould and at random the walls were studded with stained-glass windows and ancient doors stolen from temples in India and Tibet. Rather than have anything as hierarchical as an acute angle the walls flowed into each other as in an hallucination, so that it was impossible to tell where one room ended and another began, to know what was a corridor and what was a kitchen. On top of that there was a menagerie of animals who wandered in and out without restriction so that guests might be greeted by a cow in the cinema or a parrot yelling obscenities from under blankets in what probably wasn't the laundry room.

The farmhouse, set in a wooded bowl two kilometres across and accessible only by a dirt track and rough plank bridge, had, until the raid by the Guardia, been occupied by forty or so disciples of Donna's husband.

Though she was stick thin, Jennifer Carnforth only picked at her soup, salad and indeterminate 'meat in tomato sauce'.

'So, how are you feeling then, Jen?' Donna asked, trying to sound concerned.

'Oh well, you know . . . I'm a bit disappointed, to tell you the truth. My husband said that God would appear to us "Illuminated Ones" some time this year and take us all to heaven . . . but I guess that isn't going to be happening now. Which is, you know, a bit depressing for me. My husband's OK though, he loves prison.'

'Loves prison. Why?'

'He's got a captive audience and him being so charismatic he's got the whole place under his spell, even a few of the warders are secret worshippers.'

'Really? And how are you off for money?'

'It's tough. My parents won't let me get at my trust fund and the kids need all kinds of things . . .'

With a friendly expression on her face Donna said,

'I might be able to help you out there, Jen. I was thinking I could maybe look after Runciman for you.'

'That'd be terribly kind of you, Donna, but why would you?'

'Well, I've taken rather a shine to the lad, and him and my Stan are such great friends, so why not? My new partner Mister Roberts is about to come into a lot of money so I've been thinking I'd like to spread it around a bit.'

'That's awfully good of you.' Tears filled Jennifer's already watery aristocratic eyes.

'One thing I need to ask you, though, Mister Roberts – he's very keen on obedience in children. So is he obedient to adults, your Runciman?'

'Oh yes,' Lady Carnforth replied. 'If there's one thing they learn growing up in a religious cult, it's blind obedience to adults.'

'That's good to know,' Donna said, 'and he seems quite small for his age, do you think he'll grow much?'

'Oh, Donna,' the Viscountess sobbed. 'It's a terrible thing but the doctors aren't sure about that at all. The diet was so bad at the farm that they think he may never grow much bigger than a thirteen-year-old child.'

On the one hand Stanley would have liked the man on the horse to throw him some sweets, but on the other he was glad that he didn't because he considered himself more or less a teenager now and teenagers didn't eat sweets that had been thrown to them by a man on a horse dressed as an Oriental potentate. It was the evening of January 5, the festival of Three Kings, the last big party of the Christmas holidays. Tomorrow was when the children would be given their Christmas presents and the day after that, just to keep things going there was the matanza, then the day after that all the Spanish would be back at work and the Brits who were on holiday would begin to drift back to the UK and by the middle of January the village would be back to being a quiet backwater on the road to the valley of nowhere.

Next to him Pepper Fawkes showed no such inhibition and threw herself into the air to catch a handful of sweets, her T-shirt riding up to give him a tantalising glimpse of her slender torso.

For the remainder of the evening the two of them wandered through the fiesta. Occasionally their hands would brush together and they would smile shyly at each other. After an hour or so they fell in with a crowd of British kids and the whole pack, shouting and laughing and pushing hysterically, ranged over the village and the countryside, losing some of those they were with, then going looking for them, discarding others in the search, then going looking for them. Stanley hardly spoke again to

Pepper; he was just happy to be swept along amongst this crowd of kids, completely content.

Stanley was tingling with happiness when he got home around 2 a.m. and found his mother sitting in the kitchen waiting for him. Seeing her there a sense of foreboding gripped the boy, pushing his previous contentment aside as if it had never existed.

'Stanley,' Donna said in a replay of the scene they'd had in her bedroom. 'Sit down. I need to talk to you.'

The boy placed himself opposite her at the table and waited for his mother to begin speaking.

'Son. You know I love you.'

'I love you too, Mum.'

'But you are so young, how would you know what it was like to be a parent? To give everything for your child.'

As she spoke Stanley experienced another of the – what would you call it? Breakthroughs? Visions? Inevitable revelations of growing up? – that he'd been encountering lately. Stanley suddenly had the idea of life with his mother as being lived under a kind of hypnotic spell, that most of the time this person, your parent held you in thrall simply because of who they were, what they had done for you, when you were a helpless infant but occasionally, for a little while, as you got older the spell wore off and you saw them as they truly were. He had one of these moments of clarity right there in the kitchen. He knew that soon this lucidity would dissolve but for the moment he saw her as she was – a vain and silly girl, self-pitying and hysterical. She imagined the way she looked after him – dressing him in the cheapest clothes, never providing any food in their freezing cold house, making a fool of herself in the bar, recruiting him in her feuds with people who had never done him any harm – as an example of enormous self-sacrifice. Well, it didn't appear like much of a sacrifice to Stanley at that moment, it seemed like the bare minimum, if that. And now she was going to do something much worse.

Donna continued. 'You were right when you said Mister Roberts might have been sent to us as a sort of test. I don't know where he's come from but I do think he was meant especially for us, and I think the worst thing we could do with him is nothing, which is what you wanted. So the thing is . . . I've got somebody else.'

Still a bit silly from the night he'd had Stanley was slow to take in her meaning. He'd often heard her say the phrase, 'I've got somebody else.' It generally meant her previous boyfriend had been arrested or run off with their electricity money and she was now sleeping with his best mate. So he asked, 'What do you mean you've got somebody else?'

Behind Stanley there was a noise, a scraping sound, he forced himself to look over his shoulder, to see Mister Roberts descending the last couple of steps from upstairs. The big man unsteadily crossed the floor and took up a position behind Donna.

The boy stared at his mother and the robot, standing as if composed by a Regency portrait painter. Stanley was surprised that what he felt most of all after the initial shock had faded, was sorry for the two of them.

'We need to be safe,' she said.

'Is that Runciman in there?' he asked.

'Yes.'

'Hi, Runciman.' The boy waved and Mister Roberts gave a little wave back. 'He's nuts you know.'

Mister Roberts made a move towards Stanley but Donna put her hand on his arm and said, 'No!' firmly. The big man stopped in his tracks then returned to stand placidly behind Donna.

'I've told him he's not to harm you under any circumstances. And in the end you'll benefit from what we do. You'll have everything you want soon. I've got an idea now of how he should be used and soon we'll live like kings, the three of us.'

'What's to stop me stealing him back?'

His mother smiled. 'Well, you can try but Runciman doesn't mind being inside Mister Roberts like you do, so there's not going to be much opportunity for you to get in there and we'll hide him somewhere good. I'll keep guard and anyway it seems to me you're growing really fast and there's not much time left for you to fit inside him so . . .'

'You've got it all worked out then?'

'I think so. You know, Stan, I might have been a bit wild at times but I've always been there for you, nobody has ever denied that. I'm only doing this for your own good, because I love you, you know.'

'I know, Mum.' There didn't seem much else to say so he got up from the table. 'I'm going to bed now, it's late.'

'Good boy.'

'Goodnight, Mum. Goodnight, Mister Roberts.'

It seemed that's how it was with them now, they didn't fight but gave in to each other with the courtesy of Bavarian duellists.

Stanley slept well, a deep dreamless nothingness but still awoke with a snap to hear his mother and Mister Roberts leaving early the next morning. The two of them had spent the night together in her bedroom. He didn't know whether Runciman had got out of the suit or stayed in it all night, and he found he didn't really want to think about that.

However he looked at the situation he couldn't see a way in which his mother's behaviour wouldn't end in disaster, letting somebody like Runciman have control of something like Mister Roberts. It was a mistake only someone as deluded as his mum could make. Did she really think that boy would allow himself to be controlled for long?

Stanley found that he was lying there rigid with rage, sucking in shallow little gulps of angry air. Taking control of his breathing and unclenching his fists he forced himself to relax. He knew Donna had always hoped that some man would come along to rescue her, and as it turned out it looked like he was going to have to be that man. He was convinced it wasn't supposed to be this way yet it seemed like he was going to be the one who had to act like an adult.

Once he was sure the pair were gone and unlikely to return the boy got up and, putting on his warmest jacket, set off through the silent village and out into the campo. Outside his house the streets of the village were silent and carpeted with brightly coloured crushed sweets, on the window sills there were half-drunk plastic glasses of beer or sangria and paper plates with the remains of free paella on them.

Stanley took a track leading upwards to the cave where the Moors had hidden from the Inquisition and where Adey was waiting with whoever was looking for Mister Roberts.

It was a little before midnight, a few minutes prior to the day of the matanza when the brown Nissan swung into the parking place just outside the village walls. Most of the lanes between the houses were too narrow to get cars down so drivers had to park at the top of the village then walk. Donna tumbled out of the driver's seat and Mister Roberts climbed more slowly from the passenger side. Donna was full of twitchy energy. 'Jesus!' she said, stretching her back. 'What a day.'

On the other side Mister Roberts slowly closed the car door with solemn deliberation.

'Let's get the stuff out of the back,' Donna said.

Together they opened the rear of the Nissan and took out four overflowing supermarket bags. After closing up the car they carried these to Donna's house. The couple encountered nobody on the way since everyone in the village was getting an early night in preparation for the matanza.

Unlocking the door Donna whispered to Mister Roberts, 'Let's keep the noise down, Stan'll be in bed by now.'

Once inside the kitchen Donna switched on the light then, with feverish animation, tipped the contents of the bags onto the wooden table. There were mostly small denomination Euro notes, greasy and crumpled but also a tangle of cheap gold and silver necklaces, bracelets and rings. She turned to Mister Roberts.

'Do you want to get out of that thing?'

Slowly he shook his head.

'Please yourself.'

With trembling hands Donna ran her fingers over the money and the jewellery.

'Now, I'm going to pile this lot up here and this is going to be Stanley's share. He'll be amazed when he comes down and sees all this, won't he?'

After a second Mister Roberts nodded.

'I mean, after a while he'll see I did the right thing, don't you think? After I tell him what we've been doing?'

Again after a second Mister Roberts nodded.

'And you'll never hurt him?'

This time there was a longer pause before the big man moved his head slowly up and down.

'OK,' Donna said. 'Great, let's get the rest of this stuff upstairs. You know, suddenly I feel exhausted.'

The matanza dawned cold and clear. It started early for both the British and the Spanish communities but for once there was little overlap in their activities, the British either stayed locked in their homes all day or crowded into Bar Noche Azul as soon as it opened, running there with hands covering their eyes in case they caught a glimpse of what the locals were up to.

The Brits often complained that it was typical

Spanish showing off, that they couldn't kill their pig somewhere quiet but had to do it in the middle of the road where everybody could see. But Laurence sometimes wondered whether there wasn't another explanation: right up until the nineteenth century people in these parts could be burnt alive for having Arab or Jewish blood in their families so if you wanted to show everybody you had absolutely no connection with Muslims or Jews, then killing and eating a pig in the middle of the road was a pretty good way to do it.

The Spanish woke at 6 a.m. and walked or drove out into the campo to their *finca*s from where the pigs they'd been keeping all year were brought back, either trussed up in the backs of pickup trucks or dragged squealing and kicking into the village, tied by steel strings to stop them running away. A little while later the families whose pig was kept behind their house rose, and they too hauled their animals out into the street.

Waiting for them was a wooden table called a *banco* and strong men who had been deputed to lift the pig squealing onto it. Once the animal was wrenched onto the table they tried to hold it still, as if they were wrestling a naked, screaming dwarf. Next a man called the *matarife*, the slaughterman, stepped forward with a sharp knife and killed the pig with a single cut to the throat. Immediately women with bowls rushed forward to catch the blood that gushed from the dying animal's throat. This blood would later be used in the *morcillas* served to the Brits in Bar Noche Azul.

Soon the homes of all the Spanish came to resemble butcher's shops or the homes of particularly busy serial killers: rooms crammed full of basins of intestines, trays of meat, buckets brimming with blood and fresh, dripping hams hanging from the ceiling beams.

Engrossed in their work the sight of Stanley alongside the African who sold stuff around the valley, a Victorian gentleman in a top hat and a pretty Victorian lady wearing a crinoline skirt walking purposefully down the main street did not disturb them all that much. They guessed it must be some English holiday practice they hadn't come across before, that on 7 January you were visited in your home by a couple wearing fancy dress and accompanied by a black man. Still, deeply superstitious as they were, some Spaniards wondered if it was an augury that something odd was going to happen today.

In Bar Noche Azul the two TVs and the stereo were turned up even higher than usual to try and drown out the screaming of the pigs, the curses of the men and the rushing and sizzling sounds of the blow torches that were used to singe the hairs off the animals' skin. The British could do nothing to stop the smell of burning flesh and scorched hair from seeping through the tightly closed doors, except to attempt to dull their senses with drink. Every time somebody came in they would shout at them, 'Shut the door! Shut the door!'

Fabien and Armando had taken their children to see the slaughter and had left the bar in the care of a disgruntled, inefficient and lazy nephew so the *Comunidad Ingles* were having difficulty getting enough anaesthetising alcohol down their throats. For once there was not a single Spanish customer in there. Frank, Kirsten, Li Tang, Janet, Miriam, Leonard and Laurence had all arrived by eight thirty. Only Nige wasn't present, she hated the matanza so much that she'd driven to Algeciras the night before and caught the ferry to the Spanish Muslim colony of Melilla.

Donna had appeared about nine with Mister Roberts walking silently behind her. To Laurence she seemed very wound up. When the disgruntled nephew was too slow in serving her she pushed her way behind the bar, accompanied by the giant boyfriend, and they began rapidly serving everyone with drinks. The nephew thought about interfering but one look at Donna's companion rapidly changed his mind.

'Look,' she said to the boy, 'why don't you sod off

to the matanza? I'm going to pay for everybody's drinks all day, I'm sure Armando and Fabien won't mind.'

For further emphasis Donna produced from her back pocket a wad of wrinkled Euros and waved it under the boy's nose. The teenager needed no more encouragement to scuttle out of the back door, which Donna locked behind him. Turning back to the British she announced, 'Right, you bastards, let's get this party started!'

There was a momentary hesitation. Laurence rose asking, 'Donna are you sure you want to be paying for everybody?'

'Yeah, why not?' she said. 'I'm feeling generous. I've just come into a bit of money, as you can see, and I'd like to spend it on my friends.'

The lure of free drink was too strong for them. Laurence said, 'Well, all right then.'

And they all put in their orders.

La Matanza

A little while later the day was beginning to turn into another of those stop/start DVDs and Laurence was just thinking that somehow this party was a lot like the day when Mister Roberts first appeared and they'd all got drunk after dumping Sergei at the clinic in Durcal, when, seemingly simultaneous with that thought, the door crashed open and framed in the doorway was the oddest little group he'd ever seen. At the front, as if he was somehow their leader, was little Stanley looking all strange and nervous, his fists clenching and unclenching. Behind him was Adey the African merchant and behind him stood a man and a woman, who to Laurence, in his confused, drunken state, looked very similar to two characters he'd designed clothes for years back for a film about the life of the young wife of Karl Marx that had come out at exactly the same time as another film about the life of the young wife of Karl Marx. Neither film was a success though both had won awards at different film festivals in Venezuela.

The group advanced until they stood amongst the tables and chairs, halfway between the counter and the door. Detaching himself, Stanley approached the bar and picking up the remote controls which lay on top of the pile of Spanish newspapers switched off the two TVs and the stereo. In the sudden silence it felt as if they were all passengers in a speeding train that had come to an abrupt halt in the middle of the countryside. Then the sounds from outside, the screaming and the sizzling began to filter in and Miriam jumped up shouting, 'Turn up the sound! Turn up the sound! Turn the sound back on!' like an overexcited teenager whose music programme had been switched off.

'Be quiet, please, Miriam,' Adey said without turning his head.

Frank who became belligerent and racist when he was drunk, rose and weaving towards the group shouted, 'Hey, mind how you speak to a white woman, boy!'

With what appeared to be a minimum of effort the woman in the bonnet took hold of him as he passed, and with the flat of her hand pushed him back down causing his wooden chair to shatter into splinters beneath him and his head to bounce off the floor, sending Frank into unconsciousness.

This got the attention of even the most drink-sozzled; everyone stopped talking and stared at the strange quartet.

Stanley planted himself in front of his mother and Mister Roberts. 'These people, they want him back,' he said.

Donna appeared self-possessed, though Laurence noticed she kept her hands flat on the sticky bartop and her eyes flickered around the room, from the two Victorians to the gaggle of watching Brits to Mister Roberts and then back to her son.

'Not once, for a minute, did I think you'd do this,' she said.

'Let's say I'm doing it for your own good.'

Donna smiled a sad little smile. 'That's what I said to you, wasn't it? I suppose it's what everyone says. Funny though, with everybody going around doing good, how the world's so messed up.'

Stanley had thought he possessed all kinds of sophisticated arguments which he'd planned to deploy against his mother but found himself simply saying, 'He was mine. You had no right to take him.'

Rather than the hysterical shouting he was

expecting, Donna, in return, looked directly at him and asked in a calm voice, 'That's it? I took your toy away?'

'No, there's other stuff. I can't remember right now . . . It's all about . . .' With some confusion the boy looked at Adey and his two companions but they remained immobile, waiting for a signal from him. For the moment this was his play. On the way he had told them that his mother was likely to fly into a rage and they should perhaps let him try and persuade her to give up Mister Roberts without provoking a fight but now her calm had thrown him.

Laurence, struggling to understand what was going on, recalled when he had first come to live in Spain, when his understanding of the language had been quite patchy. He would read a newspaper article in *El Pais* or *ABC* and think that he'd understood it completely, certain that it was about an elephant which had escaped from a zoo in Seville and had trampled on a car, then he would read it again a little later and would be just as convinced that in fact it was about the EU and its policy towards the performing arts. This argument between Donna and Stanley was a lot like that. Constantly shifting. At one moment it seemed to be about some object that Mister Roberts possessed then a few seconds later it appeared to be about the man himself.

Donna continued, seizing the moment of her

son's uncertainty, 'After you said you were going to let me down with Mister Roberts, I understood you didn't have what it takes to help us make our fortune. I'd have to do it all myself. Honestly it's nothing to be ashamed of Stanley, being weak, but I need strong people around me, around us. I thought back to that day in Granada with the gypsies. There were so many of them and they were so fierce in looking out for each other.'

Laurence was completely perplexed by this swerve into talk about gypsies; any sense he'd had of what was going on evaporated.

Donna said, 'It struck me, that's what we needed: a big bunch of people who'd sacrifice themselves for him, for us. Where do you find people prepared to do that? Then it hit me. I mean once you think of it, it's obvious, isn't it Stan? Religion! People when they get religion, even really clever or talented people, will do the most stupid things. Footballers kiss the soil and make crosses on their chests before a game, scientists walk on their knees to Santiago de Compostella, doctors drive their cars into airport departure halls and blow themselves up.

'Now the one thing they put some effort into teaching us at school was religion. They had believers from loads of faiths come in to give us talks: there was an African who worshipped stones, a white witch who worked in telesales during the day. I saw one of our guest speakers recently on the telly, broadcasting from a cave in Pakistan.

'All these people believed just on the basis of what they had read or what someone had told them. So I'm thinking: wouldn't it be much more powerful if somebody could perform real miracles, right in front of people? That'd convert them on the spot. What wouldn't they do for you then? Get Mister Roberts in front of a mob and he would be able to do things there'd be no explanation for. You might as well call them miracles, because that's how they'd seem. Then that crowd would become his disciples. Do whatever we told them to without giving it a moment's thought. Now who would Mister Roberts' followers be?

'Well, disciples always seem to come from the dispossessed, the poor and the ugly. I guess the rich and handsome are pretty satisfied with whatever set-up they're born into.

'So who's the dispossessed around here? Not the Spanish anymore, maybe thirty years ago, but not now. The gypsies? Well, there's a problem with that. So who? Who would it be?'

As she'd gone on Donna's delivery had become more impassioned; all those in the bar, though they hadn't a clue as to what she was talking about, were transfixed by her fervour. Sometimes, when Laurence had worked on a film, he could recall witnessing a moment of pure magic. The assistant director would call action on a take which required an actor to complete a long and complex monologue. Slowly, with the camera whirring and the lights gently clicking, everybody on the set gradually got drawn into the majesty of what was happening. Of course, the words themselves played a part, the words cast a spell. But there was also something monumental in the sight of this person struggling to deliver what they had to say, while coping with so many obstacles of memory and self-consciousness. Inevitably, when they finished, the actor would receive a spontaneous round of applause. So it was with Donna's speech.

Though he still had no idea what she was going on about, as Donna continued to plead her case a majestic and demented grandeur had crept into what she was saying.

Laurence reminded himself that in the viewing theatre the next morning, when the previous day's filming was reviewed, the footage of the speech which had gained the round of applause always now appeared overblown, bombastic and fake and never made it into the final cut of the movie.

'So,' Donna continued. 'I reckon the closest we've got to Biblical slaves round here are those South Americans who work up in the *plasticas*. Think about it. They're forced from their home country, they live in terrible conditions, everybody despises them. At first I didn't know where to find any but then remembered whenever I drove to the coast with Laurence he'd go on and on about the spread of the *plasticas*.' She turned to him with a crooked smile. 'Do you remember, Laurence? You'd say you often saw little groups of them in the Latin American products aisle at Carrefour.

'So that's where we went yesterday. I half expected that they wouldn't be there, but there was a little clump of them, just like Laurence said, small brown men and women, silently fingering the packets of enchiladas.

'It's an odd thing to try and say to people you don't know, "Hello, this is God, or the son of God or God's best friend. I want you to follow him and become his disciples." I just stood there staring at the little group of Incas and they stared back.

'But at least they didn't move. It was Mister Roberts who kept them there of course, they were so small and he was so big and he has this . . . well, everybody can feel it . . . this presence.

'Do you remember? Years ago, when you landed at Malaga airport a little van would pull onto the runway, in front of the plane, with a flashing orange sign on its roof that said, "Sigame, Sigame" – "Follow me, Follow me". I just said that to them:

"Follow me". They sort of consulted together without speaking, looking at each other with their blank faces but then Mister Roberts signalled to them and they trouped off after us. We went through canned goods, household products, the fish counter, sliced meats, until we came to the salad aisle. I stopped them there in front of all the beautiful coloured leaves, crammed into their crinkly packets. "This is the fruit of your labours," I said. "You picked these salads in temperatures hotter than an oven, the air was full of poison and they paid you nothing." I indicated Mister Roberts. "And he feels pity for you. But he is also angry because you shouldn't do this work. You help them strangle the rivers and contaminate the soil. He is here to take you out of slavery. Look," I said, "look at the strength he has." Then Mister Roberts, without me even telling him to, picked up the whole lettuce section and threw it all the way into dairy products. Then the security guards came running with their batons drawn and when I looked back all the South Americans had legged it.'

Here Donna lapsed into silence giving no sign that she was ever going to continue until Stanley was forced to ask, 'So what happened?'

'Well, me and Mister Roberts drove into Granada, we waited till it got dark, broke the window of a jewellery store, robbed that, mugged a couple of tourists, and came back.'

Stanley said, 'This is mad. Look, are you going to tell him to give himself up or not?'

'No, no, no,' Donna said. 'I'm sure this religion thing could work if I just gave it another go. And we could do so much good in the world, preach a message of peace and ecology and all like that. Do you, do they, want to kill somebody who could save the planet?'

The boy didn't know what to do. He turned to the African. 'I dunno Adey, maybe she's right . . . what do you think?'

Adey put a hand on the lad's shoulder and said in a kind voice, 'Boy, your mother's crazy.'

Donna seemed at last to accept that she was not going to argue her way out of this. Squaring her shoulders she said, 'Well, from what I remember of the legends the Norse Viking told our class there's always a big battle between good and evil at some point so it looks like we're going to be having Ragnarok here in Bar Noche Azul. And from what I can see Mister Roberts is a later model than those two so perhaps he can do things they can't, we'll see won't we?'

Then turning to her companion she ordered, 'Take them, you can do it.'

Laurence was one of the few who had seen Mister Roberts using all of his physical power but even so he was staggered by the agility the big man showed as he vaulted the counter and in a half-crouch approached the Victorian couple.

If his movements were a shock, the speed and grace with which these two moved apart, throwing tables and chairs aside to give themselves more room, was just as astonishing. In a split second they flanked Mister Roberts, the woman folding her parasol with a snap, forming it into a short jabbing spear.

At the first whiff of the coming fight all of the British, following long-established practice, cleared to the walls, but for some odd reason none of them actually made for the door, which would have been the truly sensible thing to do. Laurence supposed that like him they all had a sense that they were witnessing something that they would never see again.

To Laurence the fight that unfolded resembled one of those Victorian boxing matches that went on for ninety-five rounds. In part this was due to the style in which two thirds of the contestants were dressed, but there was also something remorseless and cruel in the pounding that the three of them handed out to each other. The strangest thing, though, was that unlike all the other fights there had ever been in Bar Noche Azul none of the contestants made a sound. Apart from the smashing of crockery, the dull thud of blows and the splintering of furniture, there was silence.

The woman's spear was the first thing to make contact, jabbing up under Mister Roberts' armpit and causing him to stagger sideways.

Next, as the top-hatted man moved in, fists raised, Mister Roberts caught him with a tremendous back-handed blow sending shivers running through his body like a telegraph pole that a car has just run into. The man froze unable to move.

Donna was right, Mister Roberts was faster and stronger than his opponents but unfortunately for her his extra ability did not cancel out the man and woman's numerical advantage. The Victorian gent was not out of action for long: as Mister Roberts closed to grapple with the lady the man straightened and drove blows with his fists into the back of Mister Roberts' head. Mister Roberts threw the woman across the room, her head landing in the orange-juice-making machine behind the bar, smashing it to bits, plastic, metal and orange pulp flying everywhere.

Now Mister Roberts and the other man began trading punches. Years ago Laurence had filmed in a car factory where there had been a giant machine stamping out whole sides of cars from flat sheets of metal; their blows appeared to have as much force as that remorseless mechanism.

From behind Mister Roberts the woman re-appeared, orange juice dripping from her bonnet, and taking a good grip on his throat with one hand began to squeeze. Though he tried everything to shake her off she refused to let go and while he writhed, her other hand tore at his body with clawed fingers. From the front Mister Roberts continued to repel the man, matching him blow for blow but there were simply twice as many punches, kicks, bites and stabs coming the other way so slowly he began to crumble: first one of his arms stopped working and swung limp at his side then under assault from both of them his legs began to buckle until slowly he crumpled to his knees. The woman finally let go of the big man's neck and took the opportunity to land a tremendous blow with both fists to the top of his head. Without a sound Mister Roberts flopped face down onto the floor of Bar Noche Azul, dust, bits of prawn and peanut shells flying up into the air as he hit the tiles.

There was a pause as the Victorian man and woman stared down at their toppled foe. Then the man bent down and with a tearing sound ripped the back of Mister Roberts wide open. Gently the two of them then bent over the body and lifted Runciman out, like a giant, limp, bloody baby being born by caesarian section. The man and the woman carefully laid him on the rubble-strewn floor of the bar and looked at Adey. He stepped forward and touched his fingers to the boy's neck then ran his hands lightly over his torso.

'He's still alive,' the African said, 'but he needs to be taken to the clinic right away.'

There were a few seconds of silence before Baz started out of the trance they were all in. 'The pickup's right outside,' he said, glad to get away from all the madness. 'I'll take him.'

He, Miriam and Leonard lifted the boy and carried him out of the back door as tenderly as they could.

'Nobody must be told what went on here,' Adey called after them.

'Yeah right,' Baz shouted back. 'Who exactly do you think would believe it?'

Of course, Adey need not have worried. Besides the reticence of those in the village towards giving information to the authorities, if there was one occasion when you wanted to take a battered and bloodied thirteen-year-old to the clinic in Durcal with no questions asked it was the matanza, since a combination of sharp knives, blowtorches, drunkenness and absconding pigs meant this was their busiest day of the year and they had no time or inclination to make probing inquiries.

Donna had stayed behind the bar during the fight, now finally she came forward and the crowd respectfully parted to let her through. Slowly she knelt beside the battered form of Mister Roberts, putting her hands lightly on his torso she looked up at the Victorians and quietly asked, 'Could you turn him over please?'

They seemed to understand what she wanted and bent and rolled him onto his back.

She threw herself across him, weeping.

Laurence thought that even though her grief was perhaps real there remained a theatrical, self-pitying quality to it. Her son, who would have been justified in taking up a chair and hitting her with it, instead knelt beside her and, taking his mother's hand said, 'It's all right Mum, it's all right now, we'll be fine, I'll look after you, we don't need anybody else. After all he was only plastic and metal.'

On film sets there was generally a nurse present, often moonlighting from their regular jobs in A&E departments. One had once told Laurence that in a dangerous situation you didn't need to be afraid of people who were all spluttering and aggressive and red in the face, because all their blood was going to their head. They weren't going to do anything to you. The ones you had to worry about were those whose faces were completely white: they'd sent all their blood to their limbs prior to smacking you with them. Donna's features were the shade of the snows on Mulhacén as she looked at her son. Pulling her hand away she said, 'You couldn't stand to see me happy could you? You had to go and ruin it.'

Unlike hers, Stanley's face turned red with shame

and hurt. 'But Mum, he was just a machine. I'm your own flesh and blood.'

'He meant more to me than you ever will. After I'd done so much for other people, he was going to be my reward. He was the only one who looked after me.'

Then she collapsed again, weeping bitter tears onto the corpse of her imaginary, mechanical lover and crying out, 'Let me die here with him.'

Adey turned towards Laurence who had been trying to ease his way out of the bar without anybody seeing him.

'Mister Laurence,' he said.

'Err yes, hello?' Laurence answered, he was wedged half in and half out of the door. Outside in the street the gutters ran red with blood, men chasing runaway pigs raced past brandishing sharp knives and dismembered carcasses and miles of looped intestines hung in the doorways of all the houses opposite. Not for the first time Laurence understood why all the leading surrealists had been Spanish; if the clock overlooking the basketball court had started melting he wouldn't have been in any way surprised.

Adey said in a stern voice, 'I asked you about him and you lied to me. You swore you knew nothing, yet you must have understood how serious I was.'

'Well, I'm sorry,' Laurence blustered. 'You do know we have a rule around here that we don't tell on anybody?'

'That is a coward's way to avoid making a moral choice,' Adey stated. 'The other ones, they say they are not happy with you. That you are going to have to be made an example of.'

'That's right,' said Donna, rising furiously from the corpse of Mister Roberts, her face slick with tears. 'It's all his fault.'

Next Summer in London

It was evening in London, the gummy pavements unable to absorb even a fraction more heat exhaled it back into the atmosphere so it lay shimmering like imperfect glass over the cars, buses and the dripping pedestrians.

'Were they going to mess you up?' asked the young man.

'Well, of course I thought that's what they were going to do: mess me up in some way, smash my head in, but what they did at first seemed worse. They told me I had to look after Donna and her son. That I had to have them come and live in my big house. Adey said in his country a place the size of mine would be the airport terminal or parliament and it was criminal to keep it for just one old man.

It suited their purposes too, of course, him and his alien friends. This way somebody was keeping an eye on Donna and Stanley, making sure they didn't go around blabbing their secret.

'Though really in some ways, it was too late: the brown sauce was out of the bottle. People tell me that in the markets, around the bus stations and in the backstreets of the industrial cities where they sell stuff for the South American workers from the *plasticas*, there've started to appear on the religious stalls, alongside the crucifixes made of shells and the statues of the Virgin Mary, these painted plaster figurines of a man in a dark suit: a man with black hair, a muscular body and empty black eyes. I've seen a couple that people have brought back and I have to say the resemblance is quite remarkable. If I were to ask the South Americans directly they wouldn't talk about it but according to Nige, who of course gets on with them, the cult of the dark man is spreading through the *plasticas* like leaf mould. Though there's been no mention in the papers there have been protests, strikes, sabotage. The sect even has its first martyr, the Guardia saw to that. Nige also said that there's already been a split over the meaning of His words, as relayed by Donna. Apparently her Spanish was open to ambiguous interpretation.'

'So Donna and Stanley, they live in your house now, do they?'

Laurence paused and looked around. He wondered what he was doing in this place, he suddenly realised how tired he was, he'd had enough. And they'd had enough of him. For the last hour or so he had noticed they'd been getting nasty looks from the young man's boss. He clearly wasn't supposed to spend so long with a single person. It was time to get out of there.

'As well as saddling me with Donna they made me help dispose of the corpse. Stanley took Donna back to my house then we returned to the bar where they were pulling Mister Roberts apart. The Victorian couple and the remaining Brits, we loaded all the separate bits into my little car and drove them to the orange grove where we buried him. I had this feeling, like somebody should say something but you know, as Stanley said, he was just a machine after all. You wouldn't make a speech when you took an old stereo to the tip, would you?

'Yes, Donna and Stanley, they still live with me. It can be difficult; she's given herself permission to feel sorry for herself for the rest of her life. There's some good days when she forgets she's a victim and then she can be fun but on the bad ones there's something broken between them. It's a terrible thing to see. I mean, you get used to watching married couples going through the motions, barely concealing the hatred and disappointment that lies between them, but to see a mother and her son doing the same is painful.

'But for me it's been,' Laurence felt for the right word, 'it's been great. I told myself before it all happened that I was self-sufficient and didn't need anybody else, but now I think I was just selfish and frightened.

'You know if you go to the Middle East and you ask for directions they'll always tell you something, even if they've really got no idea where they're directing you. I always wondered why they did that, I thought they were just being annoying but now I know: to help somebody on their way, even if you haven't got a clue where you're sending them, it's thrilling! I tell Stanley all kinds of things, try and teach him all sorts of lessons and I truly think it doesn't matter if I know what I'm talking about or not as long as he knows it's done with love.

'Stanley's doing OK at school, says he wants to be a pilot one day and a plumber the next. Runciman came back too, after he got out of the hospital. He's no longer a bully. I guess getting beat up like that would put anybody off doing the same thing. In fact, him and Stanley are reasonably good mates. They share something nobody else will ever understand.

'I'll tell you something else, he goes away with Adey at the weekends to the high country. I don't go but recently people, farmers and walkers and the like, keep coming back with reports of seeing strange scaly creatures in the mountains, not just two either but a couple of little ones as well. Of course nobody believes them yet.'

Laurence looked hard at the young man. 'You know it's true, don't you? That's what I need to hear, I mean, it chimes with the things that you believe, doesn't it?'

'Well, yes, I mean, there's also some aspects that I can't square but yes, I do believe it to be true, yes. And can I say I'm very glad that you have decided you want to become part of the Church of Scientology.'

Laurence gave a yelp of laughter. 'Good Lord no!' he said, then more kindly, 'Son, I don't want any part of your religion.'

The young man looked confused and hurt. 'Then why have you been telling me all this?'

'Because I thought you'd believe it, that's all. Space aliens, who else but somebody in a group like yours would believe a story about evil intergalactic empires?' Laurence half got up from the table then paused and sat down again. 'No, I'm not being fair,' he said. 'There's another reason I chose you. When I first saw you there in the street, right away I recognised someone who was acting. I've seen enough of it and done enough of it myself. What I sensed was that you are not really a part of all this.' Laurence waved his hands around the room filled with desks at which the desperate and the confused and the

calculating sat on either side. 'I know you don't want
to feel alone, nobody does. I learnt something of the
universe over last Christmas and it is vast and cruel
and empty but I also saw that you can't hide yourself away from it. Let yourself be vulnerable, get
somebody to look after. These people, this thing,
won't fix you. Son, you need to find something that's
kinder. Here's my email . . .' Laurence said, scribbling
an address along the top of a leaflet all about stress
and how only the Scientologists could cure it. 'If you
ever want to come out I can show you a side of Spain
that the average tourist would never see. And you can
maybe meet my family. Admittedly it's not a conventional one. My immediate family is a thirteen-year-old
boy who isn't mine, plus his mother who is still
grieving for a dead robot. While my extended family
consists of a weird kid, an African and a brood of
aliens.

'But then a lot of families are very mixed up these
days, aren't they?'